MERC

THE GANGSTA... THE GENTLEMAN

B. LOVE

PROLIFIC PEN PUSHER

PREFACE

Merc was first introduced in Asylum. You do not have to read Asylum, but it's a great book, and I encourage you to do so.

PREFACE

Mood: “Safe with Me” x Sam Smith

PROLOGUE

So maybe leaving in the middle of the night wasn't the *best* idea. It wasn't my intention. Had I known Steven would give me an ultimatum—accept his bullshit or give up my home, business, and the life we were building—I would have been more prepared to make my escape. No part of my mind or heart wanted to believe the man I'd spent the last two years with could be so heartless and selfish. He knew how much music and my vinyl store meant to me; that was why he'd given it to me for our anniversary one year ago. I preferred it over an engagement ring, and now, I had neither.

It didn't matter how much I told myself it was better I get away from Steven now after seeing the real him—my heart still hurt over how the man I loved could treat me this way. It also didn't help that I had "Nothing But Love" by Lu Kala on repeat. Tears blurred my eyes as I belted the lyrics. It was as if she'd written the song just for me.

I had no real destination in mind as I drove. I could have gone to a friend's house or to my parents' home, but I didn't want to talk about what was going on with me and Steven. Under normal circumstances, I wouldn't be driving in the dark or while it was snowing.

The further I got into my drive, the worse the snow got. I'd filled up my tank before hopping on the interstate, and though I didn't check the time I started driving, since I would soon be out of gas, I assumed I'd been on the road for at least five or six hours. Unintentionally, it seemed I'd taken a familiar trail to a mountain town like Gatlinburg from my home in Memphis. Because of how windy it was and how heavy the snow was falling, I didn't want to risk driving through the mountains.

My decision not to continue driving was finalized when I got stuck in a snowdrift. I didn't think anything could make my night or my life worse, but here I was, stuck in the middle of nowhere in a huge pile of snow. Curses and cries left me as I yelled and punched the steering wheel. I was mad at Steven for betraying and abandoning me. I was mad at God for making this godforsaken snow. I was mad at myself for not paying attention to where I was driving and ending up in a snowy town so late at night.

Checking the time, I sighed at the sight of 10:39 p.m. Wiping my face, I inhaled what I hoped would be a calming breath. I tried to request a tow truck, but my insurance company's app didn't work. My outgoing calls weren't working either. If the sun was out, I'd sit in my car and hope help would drive by. Because it was pitch black out, I didn't want to risk a car coming and hitting me.

So, I got out and grabbed the two bags I packed in my car before leaving and headed north. I couldn't remember the last house I'd passed, and there were only two lights shining ahead. I had no idea what I was walking into, but anything at this point would have been better than being stuck with no service in the cold. As I headed toward the lights, I prayed they wouldn't lead to a serial killer who planned to make me their next victim.

Back in Memphis
A few weeks earlier...

NOTHING MADE me prouder than watching my son, Marz, hesitantly walk over to the little girl he had a crush on with flowers and candy in his hand. It was Valentine's Day, and he wanted to show Kiana that he liked her. When the five-year-old came to me and asked me for money to buy his girl something for Valentine's Day, I was amused. I didn't even know he was aware of doing that kind of gesture, but seeing as his mother was a hopeless romantic, I shouldn't have been surprised.

Aries told me she noticed Marz talking to Kiana every day after school, and he'd always have a smile on his face when he got in the car. Apparently, they'd been craft buddies this month, so they were working together closely on a few drawing and painting projects. I thought it was cute and was more than willing to train him young to ensure he'd be a gentleman when he grew up.

To be sure it was okay, I told Aries to reach out to the little girl's mom. After she approved of Marz getting her something for the holiday, I took my little man to the store and set him up. He made her his own love note, and the shit was so cute I took pictures of it and sent it to all my homies last night. There was truly nothing that made me happier or filled me with more pride than my son.

Both Aries and I recorded Marz on our phones as he walked over to Kiana. When she noticed him coming in her direction, she smiled. Her mouth hung open, and she clapped at the sight of everything he had for her. She took the items hesitantly and thanked him before giving him a tight hug.

"Aww, they are too cute," Aries cooed, fanning her watery eyes so her tears wouldn't fall.

Chuckling, I ended the recording on my phone.

"We doin' good with him, huh?"

"For sure," she replied, wrapping her arm around me and resting her head on my shoulder as we watched them talk for a while before they locked hands and walked into their school. "That was just too cute. I'm glad I came up here to watch."

"Same." I agreed as she released me. "What you about to get into now?"

"I'll probably go home and get a little cleaning done. I'm not sure what Omar has planned for tonight, but I want to make sure I don't have anything to do but get Marz settled before we do our thing."

If it was for any other thing, I'd offer to make sure my little man was straight so she could go out and enjoy herself. Since I didn't like her nigga, I kept my mouth shut as we walked to our separate cars. Whether I had plans or not, I'd make sure I was gone so she would either have to stay home with Marz or make that nigga come to her.

I loved Aries because she gave me my first son. People often thought we were on some sneaky link shit. I had too much respect for her to play with her emotions and make her believe there was more between us than there was. For the sake of our child, I needed to make sure Aries and I forever remained on the same page, and since my son was a year old, that page had been one of platonic friendship.

As great as Aries and I coparented, our romantic relationship wasn't as peaceful… which was why we broke up. I believed we simply didn't have enough in common to sustain a fun relationship. She was cool, though, and I was grateful we got along as well as we did. I allowed her to live in the mother-in-law suite on my land, rent free, to make sure she was straight and my son was close.

Aries didn't work, so I made sure she had enough money to take care of her other bills and still enjoy herself. A part of me hated how serious things were between her and Omar without her demanding more support from him, but she accepted a bullshit excuse about him not doing anything for her financially because they weren't married.

I didn't need another nigga thinking my little man was his responsibility, so I took great pride in providing for him and Aries, but that was the biggest reason Omar would never have my respect.

"What are you getting into tonight?" Aries asked as I opened the door of her Tesla. "Or should I ask *who* are you getting into tonight?"

That made me smile. I could admit I had a healthy sex life. Aries may have been the last woman I was in a serious relationship with, but I rotated the women I dated and had sex with regularly. Being honest though, that shit was getting kind of played out. I was tired of getting to know women and learning them. There were times I wanted one woman to know, trust, and come home to, but I didn't see that happening for me any time soon—if ever.

"I have no idea, but I know I'm getting into something."

"Yeah, I bet." She chuckled as she buckled her seat belt.

"I'm about to run some errands. Let me know when you get home."

"Okay, be safe."

With a nod, I closed her door and headed to my car. I had three. Marz wanted me to take him to school in my black Camaro because it matched his outfit. That boy was something else.

Once I was settled in the car, I checked the notifications on my phone. A smile spread my lips at the sight of Asylum's text, letting me know he was going to be a father by blood for the first time. He was on a weeklong vacation with his woman, Dauterive, and I couldn't be happier for my best friend. Out of my crew, Asylum was the one we least expected to be in a new relationship with a baby on the way... seeing as just last year he was married to someone else.

That whole situation was a trip, but I was just glad he was finally with the love of his life and still able to maintain his father daughter relationship with his stepdaughter, True. After sending him my congratulations and letting him know we'd have to celebrate when they got back, I headed out of the parking lot to run my errands for the day. I turned up the Yo Gotti that was playing and cruised the streets with peace in my soul and love in my heart... even if I didn't have a woman to give it to. My life in all other areas was good, and I was grateful to God for that.

MERC

WITH A FRUSTRATED SIGH, I rolled off Victoria. Even with the Hennessy in my system, I couldn't keep my dick hard. I kept telling myself getting it wet would keep it up, but I couldn't force myself to enter her soaking pussy. There was nothing wrong with Victoria. She was beautiful, thick, and down for whatever. It was me.

I was tired of fucking on one woman after another. The pleasure, fun, and victory of a conquest was getting played out. My mind told me because it was Valentine's Day, I deserved to end my day in some pussy, but my heart wanted something... someone... different.

Running my hand down my face, I looked down at Victoria. It was clear she was frustrated as she sat up, but she remained silent.

"Look... I'm just not feelin' this shit," I told her honestly, looking around the hotel room I'd brought her to, because I never took a woman where I laid my head and raised my son.

"Why not? Do you need me to suck you off a little longer?"

My head shook as she rubbed my back, and even her touch was annoying me.

"Nah. I think I'm just going to call it a night." Standing, I ignored the chuckle she released. "You can stay here until morning if you want."

"You're serious?" Victoria asked, watching me slip into my pants. Since that was clear by my actions, I didn't bother answering with my words. "What the hell am I supposed to do for the rest of the night, Merc?"

"I don't care. Go somewhere. Have someone else come up here. Whatever you do, it just won't be with me."

With a pout, she crossed her arms over her chest and grumbled under her breath. I did feel kind of bad for leaving her without this dick, but I didn't feel bad enough to force myself to do something I genuinely didn't want to do. Pulling out all the cash in my wallet, I set it on the nightstand and gave her a kiss on the temple. Since I hadn't gotten her anything for Valentine's Day, I told her to treat herself with the money and have a good night. Lord knows I was going to—in front of my TV with a drink... enjoying my own damn company.

My peaceful night of solitude was interrupted by Aries barging into my home. We had boundaries that allowed us to be respectful and considerate of each other since she lived behind me, so I could tell she was excited about something as she rushed into my home theater without bothering to knock or call me first. I let it slide since I wasn't entertaining anyone. Taking a swig of my beer, I kept my eyes trained on her as she skipped into the room.

"Merc!" she yelled before squealing and covering her mouth with her hands.

I took pride in being observant, so it didn't take me long to notice the ring on her left hand... her left ring finger. Scoffing, I shook my head as she came toward me.

"Omar proposed! I'm getting married!"

She stretched her arm out so far it almost hit me in my face. Chuckling, I took her wrist and lowered her hand to inspect the ring. It looked cheap as fuck, but I knew not everyone was able to spoil their woman and provide financially the way I could. Being an enforcer, for the clients I took on, was a seven-figure business. I didn't just provide security and protection; I was a hitta too. For Asylum, I was the head of his security, and I used to be a freelance musician as well. Money was something I'd never have to worry about... and neither would my son.

It was instilled in me if a man couldn't provide for his wife, he wasn't ready to be a husband yet. Still, I wouldn't speak on the cheap ring. There was an issue more pressing that needed to be addressed anyway.

Releasing her wrist, I told her, "I'on know how I feel about him being your husband."

Scoffing, she rested her hands on her waist. "What is that supposed to mean?"

"I don't like Omar. I've only tolerated him because you seemed to like him. But he ain't good enough to be my little man's stepfather, so you need to give that mane his ring back."

For a while, she just stared at me. Done with the conversation, I returned my attention to the wall. The projector was showing an *Unauthorized Biographies with Peter Graves* episode that featured John Gotti. He was probably the most influential don I'd studied over the years. Not because I was out here selling drugs or managing gambling rings or loansharking, but because of the code he lived by and instilled in his men. Even after his episode, I'd continue to watch the show because I loved learning about people who had succeeded for inspiration... regardless of how their life ended.

"I'm sorry. I'm not understanding why you think you have a say in who I marry."

"The fact that we went half on a baby gives me that right. If I don't approve of the man you settle down with, he ain't gon' be around my son."

"Merc..." My head shook as I took a swig of my beer. "You haven't really even given him a chance."

"I don't have to. He was flawed and I saw that shit in him the moment we met. The fact that he doesn't take care of you takes away even less of my respect. He hasn't proved that he's worthy of you and can take care of you, and you think I'm about to give him your hand?"

"You are not my damn daddy!"

"But I'm your baby's daddy, so that's close enough."

She huffed and pushed her hair off her shoulder. Sitting next to me, Aries took my hand into hers. I heard the shaky breath she released, but that shit didn't sway me. There wasn't anything she could say to change my view of him. Only his actions could.

"Merc, please. I love you, and I value your opinion. I respect what we've built. But if I have to choose between your approval and finally getting a man who can love and take care of me... you're going to lose."

"You that hungry for love that you willing to settle for crumbs of it?"

Our gaze stayed locked as her nostrils flared. Standing, she charged out of the room, muttering, "You're not going to ruin this for me," under her breath.

After she slammed the door, I chuckled with a shake of my head. Even if she didn't agree with me right now, there was no doubt in my mind that Aries would eventually come to her senses and give that nigga his ring back. He wasn't worth her, and I'd be damned if I let him influence my son. On the off chance she did marry him, I could only hope he was ready for war, because I was going to make his life hell by showing just how ill-equipped he was to have access to anything that belonged to me—and that included the mother of my first child.

n the other side of town...

Like I always did, I had a low playlist going while I did my makeup live. For tonight, I chose to get ready on TikTok because they hardly ever hassled me about the music that played in the background. Music was such a huge part of my life that I almost always had it playing, and when it wasn't playing, I was singing or humming a tune in my head and heart.

I didn't really talk much while I was live, so I didn't care to keep up with comments. If someone complimented me, I thanked them or offered names of products I was using for women who asked, but that was about it. I wasn't an influencer or anything; I just liked sharing one of my favorite moments with the world.

The alarm announced the opening of the garage door, letting me know Steven was home. A smile instantly spread my lips. I had no idea what he had planned for us for this evening, but I was excited for it. Since he put together our plans for the evening, I'd hired a chauffeur. I didn't subscribe to the notion that men didn't deserve effort and romance, so even though he wanted to treat me tonight, I wanted to make the evening about him too. Before he entered our bedroom, I quickly stood and stuffed his gifts in the gift bag on the bench in front of the bed.

He was stepping inside as I made my way back to my vanity.

"Hey," he spoke softly, walking over to me.

"Hey, honey. How was work?" Steven gave me a tender kiss, lowering his hand between my legs. Pushing him away gently with a giggle, I pointed to the phone. "I'm live, Steven."

"Then get off."

"I'm almost done," I mumbled as he kissed my neck.

"Listen... we're gonna have to reschedule our plans for the evening."

My smile dropped, and I gently pushed him away from me.

"What do you mean?"

Steven squeezed the back of his neck as he sat on the bench in front of our bed.

"Asia wants to do something with China tonight, and you know I can't say no to my baby girl."

Sighing, I grabbed my phone to disconnect the live. I could tell this conversation was about to get a little heated, and I didn't want hundreds of people that I didn't even know, with a few of my friends and family members sprinkled in, knowing my business.

"You're not saying no to your daughter; you're saying no to her mother."

"It's the same thing."

Chuckling, I shook my head as I set the phone on the vanity. "No, it's not. I hate to sound crass, but Valentine's Day is a day for lovers. I'm more than okay with you doing something with your daughter before we go out, but I'm not really comfortable with you not doing what you planned for us to spend time with them as a family."

His body slouched as he gritted his teeth. "It ain't really that big of a deal, Neo. Valentine's Day is a day meant to put money in other people's pockets anyway. Real couples..."

"Show their love every day," I mocked, narrowing my eyes. "That's what everyone says when they don't want to put forth the effort to make today special. But you don't show me your love every day. We haven't even been going out as much as we used to. That's why I was really looking forward to today." Twisting my mouth to the side, I inhaled a deep breath. "Like I said, I don't mind you spending some time with China and taking her something if you'd like, but I'm really not feeling you canceling our plans to spend time with them. I don't think that's fair."

"Well, baby, I'm sorry, but I'm not going to let my daughter down. Asia has already told her that I was taking them out, and I want to make sure she has the right expectations when it comes down to men, so I'm going to show up for her today."

"Let me get this straight." Releasing a low bark of laughter, I sat back in my seat. "You want your daughter to know what this day means, so you're going to take her and her mother out while your woman sits at home and does nothing... on Valentine's Day... the day for lovers." When he didn't respond, my laugh grew louder. "Go ahead, Steven. I'm not going to beg you to honor the plans you made for me."

"Come on, Neo. Don't make this a thing."

Ignoring him, I sat forward and continued to do my makeup. I didn't want to show my hurt over his actions. I hated feeling like a bitter woman who didn't want him spending time with his daughter, because that certainly wasn't the case. I felt robbed, more than anything. What I'd said was true—we hadn't been spending a lot of time together. He'd been promising me that today would be the start of us getting back on track. Now, he expected me to be okay with him canceling our plans to be with his daughter and her mom.

Hell, I would even feel better about it if he got China and brought her here with us. However, something about him including Asia wasn't sitting right with me. I had no reason to believe he was still messing off with his baby mama, but she was single, and I felt like she was using their daughter as a way to get Steven to treat her this evening instead of me. If that was the case, it would have been a waste of my time trying to get him to see that.

"You're going to ignore me now?" he continued, pressing his palms together between his spread legs.

"You've made it clear how it's going to be, so we don't have anything else to talk about."

"Yeah, but I don't want you to feel like you don't have a say."

"I don't," I replied with a chuckle. "You have decided to spend the evening with them, and I'm not included in that. What say do I have?"

He sucked his teeth. "I just didn't think you'd want to spend the evening with us."

"That's fine, Steve."

My tone was clipped, and I hoped he dropped it. It was bad enough he'd ruined our plans for the evening. I wasn't trying to argue tonight too. Grabbing my phone, I decided to call my best friend, Innvy, and see if she wanted to do something tonight.

"Hey, boo," she greeted after answering, and I could hear the smile on her face.

"Hey, babe. What you doing?"

"Nothing right now. I was thinking about going out to eat, but I know everybody gonna be packed tonight."

"Right. Well... we can hit up a bar or something. That'll probably get us quicker service than a restaurant."

"Wait. What happened to your plans with Steve?"

"We'll talk."

"Oohwee. Okay. You come over here and we can Uber so we can drink drink."

Laughing, I nodded my agreement. "Okay. I'll text you when I'm on my way."

After disconnecting the call, I canceled the driver I'd requested for tonight then returned my attention to my face. I would have kept it, but an Uber was cheaper. I was almost done; I just needed to add my blush and set my face.

"I guess I'ma head out since you're ignoring me."

"Okay, be safe."

Chuckling, Steven left the room with a shake of his head. As soon as I heard the garage door slam, I had to keep myself from crying. As much as I loved him, I was losing more and more resolve and interest when it came down to our relationship. Things were so good between us, and now, it seemed like he was changing right before my very eyes.

It didn't seem to matter if I brought things I didn't like or weren't comfortable with to his attention. If he didn't agree, it wouldn't change. Love was starting to not be enough to keep us on solid ground, and as much as my heart didn't want to admit it, it was probably best for me to start getting ready for things between us to end.

As Innvy and I prepared to leave, the man I'd been talking to for most of the evening wasn't letting up. His friend was shooting his shot with Innvy and we, Merc and I, ended up talking while they did their thing. Merc wasn't flirting with me, but he made it clear he didn't respect the fact that I had a boyfriend and was spending the evening with my girl. Now that I was trying to pay my bill, things were becoming clearer. Not just with Merc... but with Steven too.

"Merc, please," I said, trying to remove the ticket from under his large, tattooed hand. "I can pay for this myself."

"I know you can, but I'm not letting you. It's bad enough you got somebody claiming you who got you here for Valentine's Day instead of with him. The least he could do is pay for you and your girls' drinks."

"I'm sure he would if I asked."

Merc chuckled, and I couldn't deny how sexy it was. What was even sexier was the fact that he didn't try to make something happen between us, even though we were attracted to each other. We kept the conversation casual, and I truly appreciated that.

"Aight, I'll make you a deal." He licked his lips and flipped his hand, connecting his fingers with mine. "Call ya man and if he pays, I'll leave you alone. If he doesn't, you have to break up with him."

"That sounds like a good idea to me," Innvy said, not making this any easier.

Usually, I wasn't the kind of person who felt I had to prove anything, but a part of me wanted to see if Steven was willing to at least take care of the bill since he couldn't take me out. So, I agreed, but decided to text him instead of calling.

Honey, Innvy and I are getting ready to leave the bar. Will you take care of the bill since we didn't go out tonight?

"There." I set my phone on the table. "I hope y'all are happy now."

Chuckling, Innvy swirled the last of her water around in the glass. We'd kept it simple for the evening, sipping tequila while the guys alternated between whiskey and beer, but when we started to wind down, we both opted for water.

"I'll be happy when you leave Steven."

"I thought you liked him?"

"I did when he was treating you right." My eyes rolled as I huffed. "I love you, and I love spending time with you, but you should've been with your man tonight, not me."

Before I could respond, my phone lit up and vibrated on the table. Innvy grabbed it quickly as Merc asked her, "What it say, sis?"

"Oof." Her head jerked and eyebrows raised. "Give that man your number, boo," was what she said, putting my phone face down on the table.

I refused to believe Steven said no, so I grabbed it, and Merc read the text with me.

Honey: I'm already paying for Asia and China. I'm not paying for you and her too. Take care of that shit bae. I got you when WE go out.

With a shake of his head, Merc put two hundred-dollar bills on top of the receipt, which was more than enough to cover all of our drinks. Gently, he took my phone out of my hand. Before I could stop him, he was leaning closer, wrapping his arm around my shoulders, and taking a picture of us. I couldn't stop my body from reacting to his closeness. He smelled so damn good, and my nipples hardened from the heat of his body being so close to mine.

Merc sent it to Steven and texted him, *don't worry about it bruh. I got her.*

"Merc!" I yelled as I punched his shoulder. Innvy's laughter only pissed me off more as my heart raced. "Why would you send that! Now he's going to think I'm cheating on him."

"Nah, he's going to think he has competition, which will make his ass act right," Merc countered. "It's fucked up you have to do that, but maybe he needs a reminder of who and what he has in you."

He shot me a wink and smile as my eyes watered.

I couldn't even bring myself to argue with him. Innvy reserved our Uber as silence found me. Merc didn't say anything else, which I appreciated. When our Uber driver arrived, the guys walked us out. Innvy promised to call Merc's friend, which sucked, because that meant I'd be seeing him around.

I wasn't sure what hurt worse—the fact that Steven didn't even bother to respond to the picture of me and Merc, or if Merc had spoken the truth. I *did* deserve better, and it was getting harder and harder for me to ignore that.

As I prepared to spend the evening with my guys, Bully was being as big of a gossip as a woman. I could only chuckle as he told me about Innvy. Apparently, he liked her more than he was able to admit right now. Bully, born with the name Gabriel, was a retired basketball player who was enjoying living a slower and more relaxed life. He did security with me and Asylum when he wanted to busy himself doing something active, but other than that, he spent his days traveling or mentoring and coaching young men at various schools in Memphis.

"I'ma see you a lil bit later, though," I told him, wrapping my Rolex around my wrist.

Aries said she wanted to talk before I headed out, and I knew she'd be coming in soon.

"Aight, bet. I'ma see if Toe coming out tonight too."

"Do that. I feel like I ain't seen him all year."

"I don't think we have. I'll let you know what he says."

"Aight, cool." I agreed before disconnecting the call.

Out of our crew, Beethoven was the only one still in the streets. He was always on go with his father and cousin, so we didn't see him as much as we used to. Now that Dauterive was back in Asylum's life, he spent a lot of his time with her and True. I could respect and understand that because I was on the same wave with my little man, but I always made sure both Aries and I took time outside of the house. We were more than parents, and I never wanted us to lose ourselves in our son.

The day was going to come when he left us and started doing his own thing, and we'd have to still live life. Because of that, it was important to me that we not only raised him in a way that would allow him to be a healthy, independent man, but that we continued to care for ourselves and keep up with our lives and identities too.

A few minutes later, Aries was ringing the doorbell on the back door that I'd installed. I yelled for her to come in, and the sound of Omar's voice had my jaw clenching as I pulled in what I hoped would be a calming breath. He was one person that truly irritated my spirit, and I really prayed Aries saw the real version of him before she tied herself to him for life.

I think her situation was what made me handle the young lady at the bar the way I did last night. After hearing Aries's news, I decided to go out for drinks with Bully. When he noticed Innvy, I agreed to keep her girl company while he did his thing. Neo was beautiful, but I wasn't in a place to try and make anything happen with her. Though I wanted something different and had left Victoria because of it, being a father and my work kept me too busy to try and start anything serious right now.

After hitting my outfit with a few sprays of Mont Blanc Legend Spirit, I headed down the hall and met them in the living room. Aries was laughing at something Omar said, but her smile faded at the sight of me.

"You look nice," she complimented. "Where are you getting ready to go?"

I looked down at my all-black attire absently before giving her my attention. "Thank you. And I'm not sure yet. Somewhere with the guys."

"Cool, well, Omar and I wanted to share some news with you."

"Wassup?" I asked, sitting in the recliner that was to the left of the couch they were sitting on.

"I'm pregnant."

Omar put his hand on her knee. The crooked grin he gave me made me want to cut his lips off. He didn't deserve to put his dick in the same space that gave birth to my son. I didn't want to be in a romantic relationship with Aries, but I'd protect her forever off the strength of my son... and that included her heart.

I was struck breathless before I grunted a laugh. This just kept getting better and better. "So he didn't propose because he loved you; he proposed because you're pregnant?"

"Of course he loves me," Aries said, but I didn't really care about what *she* had to say. I wanted to hear his response.

"Do you?"

"Yeah, I love her. But I can't lie, if she wasn't pregnant, I wouldn't have proposed."

My head shook as I stood. This was too reminiscent of Asylum and Sierra. He married her because of a child that wasn't even his and was miserable because of it. It took him twelve years to get back to the woman he was supposed to be with.

"Look, I can't tell you what to do," I said, locking eyes with Aries. "I just hope you know what you're getting yourself into. This ain't giving what you think it is. You can do a hell of a lot better than him."

The grin that had been on Omar's face fell as he stood. Aries stood as well, taking his hand into hers.

"I thought you'd be happy for me. You won't have to take care of us anymore. Isn't that a good thing?"

"It's literally nothing for me to provide for you and our son. If that's why you're doing this, you know you don't have to do that."

"I'm marrying him because I love him, Merc, and I hope one day that's enough for you." She paused and exhaled deeply. "Omar is taking me to Mississippi to meet some of his family, and I'm going to take Marz if you didn't have anything planned for him this weekend."

A quick no jerked my head. I headed out of the living room, knowing they would follow me. I was done with this conversation. She wasn't going to heed my warning until Omar started revealing his true self. Until then, if she was okay with his bare minimum ass, that was on her.

"Nah, you can take him." I looked at Omar as I added, "Take care of my son. If anything happens to him, I'll kill you."

Aries groaned and gently shoved Omar in the opposite direction toward the back door. She knew there wasn't anything he could say to soften me toward him. I didn't play when it came to Marz, and if she was dead set on keeping Omar in his life, he would be held to the same standard of keeping him safe as I held myself.

"WHATCHU THINK ABOUT NEO?" Bully asked with a wide grin.

"Neo?" Beethoven repeated, sitting up in his seat.

We'd gotten a booth at Tyreek's gentlemen's club for the evening. The blue lighting and dark ambiance were always a relaxing vibe. Tonight was more of a networking night, so there wasn't a live band or strippers to entertain. I respected the atmosphere that Tyreek had created here. It was a fun, safe vibe for professional men over thirty that the city needed.

"Shorty from the bar last night," I replied. "And I think nothing of her other than she's a beautiful woman in a relationship she don't need to be in."

Bully chuckled. "You think more than that."

My head shook as I avoided both their eyes. Taking a sip of my whiskey, I couldn't keep myself from smiling. Neo was beautiful, that I wouldn't deny. I had a bad ass habit of trying to save women who didn't want to be or couldn't be saved. I guess it came from being raised by a real man and being one myself. Any time I heard a woman was in need, it was my instinct to try and rescue her. I'd learned long ago, though, that a man trying to come between a woman and the man she loved, no matter how toxic the relationship or abusive the man was, would always be the enemy.

"Hol' up, so this is someone he tried to get at?" Toe clarified.

"Nah," I answered, setting my glass down. "I was keeping her company while he got at her girl. And from the sound of it, his ass sprung already."

My deflection worked because that caused Beethoven to start asking Bully questions about Innvy. When our waitress came back to the table, I ordered smoked wings and fries. We spent the rest of the evening catching up before parting ways, and I was glad we had an early night. I wanted to spend as much time with my little man as I could before he left for the weekend.

One Week Later

As happy as I was to see a familiar face, I was also nervous. I didn't want Merc asking me about my relationship. Truth was, things hadn't gotten better between me and Steven. Two years together and we were crumbling. To Steven's credit, he got me some nice gifts for Valentine's Day the next day, but that made me feel like the side chick. We were supposed to go out this past weekend, but I had to work. I only had one employee at my vinyl store, and she had been out sick.

Crazy thing was, Steven didn't give a damn about me pulling double shifts all weekend. All he did was ask me if I was going to cook so he'd have something for dinner while I was gone. Bully and Innvy were hanging out when I Face-Timed her to vent, and before I got off the phone, I gave her a brief rundown of how busy my weekend was going to be.

Bully told Merc, and he had breakfast, lunch, and dinner delivered to the store for me the entire weekend.

The gesture made me cry. Even without Merc's presence, his energy spoke volumes. He was considering me and taking care of me better than my man was, and Merc and I didn't know a thing about each other. Having him come into my store today made me feel bad. How would I explain why I was still with a man that I clearly needed to break up with? It didn't seem to matter, because Merc was in the back of the store pacing, on what looked to be a very heated call.

I'd been entertaining the older man he'd come into the store with. His name was Rey, and he was pretty cool.

"I didn't even know this store existed," Rey said, holding a vinyl version of an Otis Redding album that I didn't want to part with. It was the only one I had, and I played it in the store, but if he wanted it, I'd let him have it. "Merc told me about it because we both love music. He loves to play, but I love to listen."

My eyes found Merc, and I grew concerned because of his angered expression.

"Does he? I didn't know we had that in common."

"Yeah, he'd probably never just tell you that." Rey chuckled. "He's... a very guarded individual. He doesn't talk about himself."

"Hmm... good to know."

We continued to talk, mostly about the wide range of vinyl records in my collection. Rey couldn't believe I had so many blues and jazz legends that were hard to come by. I could tell he was impressed, and that filled me with pride.

My eyes lifted as the front door opened. I was about to speak and tell the customers I'd be with them soon, until I realized they weren't customers. They were robbers in black masks. Dropping the vinyl record I was holding, I gasped. My eyes widened when I realized they were aiming their guns directly at Rey.

Were they here for him?

"Rey, look out!" I yelled, but it was too late. Bullets began to pierce the air, and one of them hit him instantly. He fell forward, and I grabbed him, pulling him behind the shelf with all my might.

The gunfire caused Merc to spring into action. He shoved his phone into his pocket and pulled out a gun, telling me to stay down and keep Rey from getting up.

My eyes closed, and I covered my ears as rapid gunfire sounded off. Body shaking, I prayed that God would spare all our lives. There might have been some things about my life that I was unhappy with, but I didn't want it to be over any time soon. At the feel of hands gripping my arms, I shook. My eyes popped open, and relief filled me at the sight of Merc.

"I got two of them, but one got away. You need to come with us."

"What? I-I can't just leave my sto—"

"Them not the kind of shooters to leave any witnesses, Neo. You need to come with me. *Now*."

Before I could protest any further, Merc was lifting me off the floor like I was a rag doll that weighed less than a pound. He tossed me over his shoulder and carried Rey out bridal style. Tears filled my eyes as drops of blood hit the floor from Rey's body.

Who the fuck were these men, and what had their presence in my store gotten me into?

One phone call from Aries and I was knocked off my square. She called me talking about how much she loved spending time with Omar's family and loved how well they interacted with Marz. Then, she had the nerve to fix her mouth and say she wanted to move with him to Atlanta. I told her that was cool as long as she knew Marz was going to stay here with me, and she didn't agree. I was so caught up in going back and forth with her regarding where my little man would be staying that I wasn't paying attention. Because of that, I failed at my job to keep Rey safe.

I didn't want to take the job to begin with. Marz changed me. I wanted less dangerous jobs to avoid being taken away from him. The odds were already stacked against me as a Black man in Memphis. I didn't want to jeopardize my life even more, offering my services to the wrong people. Originally, I was going to decline Rey's request for protection. He was honest with me and told me his old best friend and business partner was trying to push him out of their business and threatened to do whatever it took to get Rey out of the way.

My OG, Supreme, asked me to work with Rey on his behalf, and that was the only reason I agreed. If I had it my way, I'd stop offering my services personally and train men and women on not just the physical part of protection, security, and enforcing, but the mental and emotional aspects of it as well. That was my goal—to be training and not offering my services personally—by the time Marz was old enough to understand what it was I actually did. Because I would never tell him that sometimes my job required me to take the lives of others.

I was grateful Neo noticed the men when she did. If she hadn't, they probably would've hit Rey more. Thankfully, he'd only taken one bullet to his side. The pain pills his doctor had him on knocked him out, but when he woke up, he asked to speak with me. I made my way into his bedroom, and the sight of him weakly lying in bed with an IV in his arm made me feel like shit. While I would never regret putting my son first, I shouldn't have answered Aries's call while I was out with Rey, unless it was for an emergency. That conversation could have waited, especially if she knew it was something that would frustrate me.

"Where's Neo?" he asked as I made my way over to his bed. He never wanted to go to a hospital for a situation like this, so I was glad his home was as large as it was. All of his guards were able to have their own space but still be near if he needed them. "Is she okay?"

"She's fine physically. She's upset that she has to be here, and she's confused about what's going on." I shrugged as I sat in the chair next to his bed by the night-stand. "Scared, I suppose."

"Have you told her anything about what's going on?"

My head shook. "It ain't my place to tell your business."

Rey chuckled, but it turned into a grimace. "I figured Bart would have his men following me, but I didn't think he'd have them shoot in broad daylight, especially with innocent bystanders around."

"Well, today has proven just how serious he is about getting you out of the way." I paused before adding, "Listen, I apologize for not being on top of things. After I checked the exits in the store, I should have stayed by your side."

"What was that about anyway?"

"My baby mama called, talking about moving my son to another state. I shouldn't have answered a personal call while I was guarding you."

"Did you handle them?"

"I got two. The last one was able to get away, but he was hit. I have my connects at all hospitals waiting for a gunshot victim that fits his description."

Rey nodded his agreement. "We need to secure that location. If the police know there was a shooting there, they are going to want know why, and I can't have them looking into my business to figure out why Bart would want me out of it. For all intents and purposes, we run a simple luxury bus and truck fleet company, and it needs to stay that way."

"I already have that taken care of. The scene has been cleaned, and Neo's security cameras have been cleared. I couldn't get the ones from surrounding businesses, but surprisingly, none of her neighbors even came out to see what was going on."

"That doesn't surprise me. I wonder what the hell she's doing in the heart of the hood anyway." He shifted, and discomfort covered his face. "Line the guards up and bring Neo in here for me. It's time I let her in on what's going on."

I did as he asked, holding back a smile at Neo's irritation. Her eyes rolled and nostrils flared as she passed me, bumping into me with her shoulder in the process.

"You mad?" I asked as she made her way down the hall like she knew where she was going.

"I've been trapped in that room for hours. Of course I'm mad."

"Look," I called softly, grabbing her wrist. Pulling her closer, I forced myself not to get lost in how beautiful she was. I'd been distracted enough for the day, and it almost cost her and Rey their lives. I couldn't afford to be distracted again. "I'm sorry, aight? I just... figured it was best to give you your space. That was a lot to take in."

"What the hell was that about, Merc? Those men could have killed him." She chuckled as her eyes watered, and she looked away. "They could've killed *me*." Her head hung. "You saved my life," she whispered.

"Yeah, but it shouldn't have even been on the line. That was my fault." Lifting her head by her chin, I made sure to tell her, "That will never happen again."

Swallowing back her emotion, her head bobbed softly. There was something about the softness and tears in her eyes that unnerved me. When it became too much, I took her by the hand and led her into Rey's room. The other five guards on the premises were already here. Two remained at both doors for safety reasons but would be updated after the meeting.

I made my way back to Rey's side since I was the head of his security, though I didn't feel like I even deserved to be at this point. True enough, there was no doubt in my mind I was the most lethal man in this room, but my personal affairs got the best of me today. Even though Rey seemed to understand, that was unacceptable.

"I am deeply regretful about bringing that violence to

your store," Rey said to Neo as she avoided his eyes and twiddled her thumbs. It was clear she was uncomfortable. "Merc has assured me that your store has been taken care of, which is the good news."

She locked eyes with him as she asked, "And what's the bad news?"

"Unfortunately, you're now a target."

Scoffing, Neo clutched her chest. "Me? How am I a target?"

"Until the last shooter is found and taken care of, he can come back for you. He knows where to find you. You'll need to stay here until he's handled."

Neo chuckled, and her head shook as she lifted her hands. "I'm sorry, but no. You're cool, but I don't know anything about you. I'm not staying here."

"If you don't want to stay here, you can stay at a hotel or something, but you'll need to be guarded. Regardless, I'm not advising you go home or to your store until he's found. I'm truly sorry about this, Neo, but it's for your own good."

Her eyes lifted to the ceiling as she quietly talked to herself.

"You'll be protected," Rey assured her. "You won't have to stay here twenty-four-seven, but a guard will have to be with you when you leave. I'm not going to let anything happen to you, because you helped me."

"You promise I won't be trapped here?" she confirmed.

Rey nodded. "I do."

"Is it going to take a long time for him to be found? I don't want him ever coming back to my store, but I'm not trying to stay here for long."

"I can't give you a timeframe, but Merc's connections work pretty fast."

Swallowing hard, Neo looked from the line of large, expressionless men who stood behind her to me.

"Can it..." Her mouth shut and small hand trembled as she pointed at me. "Can I have him?"

Neo's request had me gritting my teeth as I fought back a smile. If I was a puppy waiting to be adopted, my tail would be wagging as I ran circles around her. I couldn't believe she trusted me with her life and safety after what happened. But the fact that she did had my heart expanding in size like the Grinch.

The fuck was this woman doing to me?

Neo

As crazy as my day had been, I didn't have the energy it took to be upset with Steven. When Merc brought me home to pack a few bags, I tried to wait for Steven to tell him what had happened. I'd already informed my employee that the store would be closed indefinitely. I'd called my parents and Innvy to let them know what was going on as well. Even though they all were worried and grateful I was okay, they told me to do as Rey and Merc said to ensure I'd be safe. Steven was the only person I'd been unable to get ahold of, and I could tell he hadn't been home from work, though he got off three hours ago.

When I got tired of waiting for him, I decided to tell him about what happened on his voicemail since he wasn't answering his phone.

"This isn't the kind of thing you leave on someone's voicemail, but since you're not answering, I have no choice." Huffing, I turned my back to Merc, though he would still be able to hear me, as he stood at the doorframe with his head tilted and arms cupped. "There was a shooting at the store. I'm fine, but I have to go into a bootleg witness protection until the last shooter is found. I guess I'll see you when I see you."

After disconnecting the call, I shoved my phone into my purse. I didn't want to suggest I'd be able to move around freely. For a while, I wanted Steven to hear my message, think he wouldn't be able to see me, and suffer. Yes, it was petty, but that's what his ass would get for not answering my calls. Literally, anything could have happened to me, and he would have no clue. Today was proof to me that he wasn't dependable, and I questioned if he even cared. Not wanting to focus on my horrible relationship, I muttered, "I'm ready."

I grabbed my bags, but Merc took them from my hands. I expected him to say something slick about Steven, but he remained silent, which I appreciated. When we made it to the front door, he told me to hang back while he took my bags out and made sure no one had followed us here. Once he was confident it was safe for me to come out, he came to get me, and we made our way to Rey's house. I still hadn't fully processed everything that had happened today, and I wasn't sure how I'd react when I did.

"Why did you choose me?" Merc asked.

"Seemed like the natural thing to do," I replied without much thought. "I know we don't really know each other, but you're the only one I felt comfortable with outside of Rey in that room. Plus, you're nice. And you saved my life already. Why wouldn't I choose you?"

Merc didn't answer me, and I was okay with that. It seemed we both had a lot on our minds that we needed to work through.

After getting a tour of Rey's mansion, I was able to choose a room. I chose the one that was closest to Rey's room. He assured me that there would always be guards here and that we would both be protected. Merc wouldn't be here always, but if and when I needed to leave, he would be with me. That was good enough for me. Unlike when I first arrived, the mansion wasn't filled with men. There were several outside and only two inside.

Once I had my bags secured, I made my way outside, hoping the darkened sky would help soothe me before I took a shower and tried to get some sleep... though I was sure I wouldn't be able to get to sleep any time soon.

The weight of the day finally got to me, and I released my tears. I hadn't meant for anyone to catch me in such a vulnerable state, but that seemed to be the case when the sliding door opened. Quickly wiping my tears, I turned as my body crumbled more. Now that they'd finally started to flow, I couldn't stop them or my sobs. When the body sat next to me, I knew by the cologne that it was Merc. He pulled me into his side and held me as I cried. When the sobs turned into whimpers, I pulled away and wiped my face.

"Why you cryin'?"

His simple question and nonchalant tone made me laugh. My life had been upended temporarily, and I was trapped in this compound of a mansion with no one I really knew. Men were shooting in my store, near me, and I saw a man almost lose his life. Yet, here he was, asking me why I was crying, as if this shit was normal. Maybe it was to him. As effortlessly as he aimed and shot, Merc clearly knew what he was doing.

"I'm scared," I admitted.

Merc's hand hovered over mine for a second, as if he was battling with whether he wanted to touch me or not. Finally, he gave in, and I was glad he did when the warmth of his hand covered mine.

"Look at me," he commanded. I did. "As long as I'm here, you don't have anything to fear. You're under my protection now, and that means I'd even go to war wit' God behind you." Merc chuckled. "Trust me... it ain't shit that nigga will be able to do to you."

I trusted him, maybe more than I should have, so I nodded.

"So what are you? A bodyguard or something?"

"Or something," was his answer, making me smile. "Providing protection is a part of what I do."

"What else do you do?"

His eyes shifted toward the sky. "I don't think it matters anymore. Rey is going to be my last client. After him, I'm done."

Nibbling my cheek, I wondered how deep I wanted to go. It seemed he didn't want to offer up a lot of conversation, but seeing as he was the only person here I was comfortable talking to outside of a sleeping Rey, I decided to talk for as long as Merc would allow.

"Is today why you want to quit?"

"It's not the reason, but it is confirmation that it's time."

"Well, thank you again for saving both of our lives. I don't know what Rey is into to need this kind of protection, but he's lucky to have you."

Merc scoffed with a shake of his head. "So lucky he's laid up in bed with a shot to the side?"

"It could have been worse." When he didn't respond, I continued. "Is Merc a nickname because of what you do?"

That made him smile genuinely. "Yes and no. I'm known in the streets as Merc because it's short for mercenary, but it's also short for Mercury, which is my government name."

"Mercury," I repeated, leaning more into his side unintentionally. "That's beautiful and unique." He looked at me, smiling with his eyes though his expression remained one of stone. "Can I call you that?"

"No one calls me Mercury." His eyes lifted back to the sky. "But you can call me that."

A smile lifted the corners of my mouth.

I feel special.

We sat outside for a while longer, looking up into the sky silently. When I started to get tired, I excused myself and retired to my room. After my shower, I took a couple of the Advil PM pills I'd brought, hoping they would help me go to sleep. I checked my notifications, and my eyes rolled at the missed calls from Steven. I started not to call him back, but that would make me just as bad as him.

He answered almost immediately with, "Where you at, and what happened at the store?"

"I told you what happened on the voicemail I left you."

Steven sighed. "Are you okay, bae? Did someone try to rob you? Where you at?"

"I'm fine. I was shaken up, naturally, but I'm okay now. No one tried to rob me. They were shooting at a customer in the store. And I don't know where I am, honestly, but I'm safe."

"Can I come see you?"

My head shook as if he could see me. "No. I'm not

allowed to give anyone my location, but I can come see you. I'll just have to have a guard."

"Okay. Tomorrow?"

"We'll see," was what I settled on. While a part of me was glad he seemed concerned, I was kind of over him for the day. I knew he wouldn't tell me what he was doing earlier and why he was unable to answer my calls, so I didn't bother asking. We talked for about thirty minutes or so, until the pills kicked in. And I was grateful they were strong enough to put me to sleep.

That Friday

I took Marz to school, and Aries picked him up. That had been our routine since Marz started kindergarten last August. This morning was a bit more difficult for me because I wouldn't see him again until Monday. I fixed his favorite breakfast, and we ate it together before it was time for us to leave.

When I pulled into the school parking lot, I told him, "Aight, little man. Are you excited about your trip this weekend?"

"Yes, sir." He confirmed with a nod. "Mommy said I'll get to see some cows."

That made me smile. "You will. I want you to have fun, but be good, okay? And if anyone does or says anything that makes you uncomfortable or is on the bad chart at home, call me."

"Yes, sir."

I really didn't want to let him go, but I knew I had to. Him spending the weekend with my or Aries's parents in the city was one thing, but him leaving the state was altogether different. Mississippi wasn't too far away, so if he needed me, I could get to him quickly.

I got out of the car and went to his side to open the door. After giving him a hug and letting him know that I loved him and would miss him, I let him head into the school. They were going to leave as soon as they picked him up today, and I had faith that Aries would take care of my son. She was a good mother; it was just her attraction to and love for Omar that had me questioning her lately.

Once he was inside, I left and headed to a couple of stores. Before leaving Rey's mansion yesterday, I sparked a casual conversation with Neo to get an idea of what her hobbies and interests were. I could tell she was going a little stir-crazy being in the house. When she first got there, she was adamant about being able to leave. For the last two days, it didn't seem like she wanted to. I hoped it wasn't because she was scared, but I couldn't blame her if she was. I tried to assure her that she was safe with me; however, based on how things went at her store, I could understand if we still needed time to build that trust.

It took me about two hours to grab everything before I headed to Rey's. When I arrived, I checked in with the guards and checked on Rey before making my way to Neo's room. Rey told me she'd been out long enough to have breakfast with him and work out outside before she went back into her room. He said she'd been closed off a lot, which I understood. She didn't feel comfortable with anyone but us. I limited the guards inside the home so she'd feel more comfortable roaming around freely.

I hated the situation we'd put her in, but I was working

to get it taken care of as quickly as possible. As soon as the third shooter was found, she'd be able to return home. True enough, there was no guarantee Bart wouldn't send anyone else after Rey, but I didn't think he'd come after her once we made an example out of his men. What was even worse was the last shooter was his son. I didn't know if that would make him go harder or stand down, but I'd make sure my team and I were prepared either way.

My knuckles tapped against the door softly. She released a low huff that made me chuckle before saying, "Come in." Neo was cute. She was sweet but easily irritated. She didn't seem to take shit from anyone except her man.

When I stepped inside, she smiled.

"Hi," she almost whispered.

"Why you locking yourself up in this room?"

Neo shrugged, eyes lowering to the basket in my hands. "Is that for me?"

"It is." After setting it on the bed in front of her, I told her, "I'm sure you're probably bored in here since you're staying in this room, so I got you a few things to entertain you."

She said she liked reading and embroidery, so I grabbed her a few books from Walmart and the stuff the lady at Michael's said she'd need to embroider—whatever the fuck that was. I added some games too, solo and multiplayer.

"Aww, thank you, Mercury."

After going through everything, she stood and gave me a lingering hug. She smelled good. She felt even better. Clearing my throat, I gently put some space between us. Neo's body was too soft to be pressed up against mine for too long.

"You're really nice. I'm glad you're here while I'm going through all this."

With a chuckle, I shook my head. "Stop calling me nice."

"Why? You are nice."

"Neo..."

"You paid for me and my girl's drinks, you had food delivered to my store, and now you're doing this for me. If that's not you being nice, what is it?"

"Being nice isn't sincere. I'm kind and I'm generous, but I'm not nice."

Her eyes rolled as she looked toward the ceiling with a smile, causing her thick locs to fall from her shoulders to her back.

Neo was absolutely beautiful.

She had cocoa brown skin and a curvy medium build that I'd admittedly dreamed about having next to mine. Her shoulder length locs were shaped to frame her diamond shaped face. Slanted light brown eyes and round, pouty lips added to her feminine appeal. If I was fucking off like I used to, I would've *been* sampled her pussy. But Neo was the kind of woman who gave off an aura that you'd want more.

My life wasn't built to indulge in more. Even though my heart wanted it, situations like this were proof I couldn't have it. Not only was I fully devoted to my family, but my career came after that. It wouldn't be fair of me to ask a woman to settle for so little of my time and effort... and I didn't think there was a woman alive who could earn my priority. I had too much loyalty to the things I was passionate about for that. That was why, up until now, I was cool with friends with benefits. It was unfortunate that was no longer enough.

"Well, thank you for your kindness and generosity. Is that better?" she asked, returning her eyes to mine.

"You're welcome."

I turned to leave, but I stopped when she asked me, "Um... do you... have plans for the day?"

"I do, actually. I have a lead on where Gatlin, the third shooter, is hiding while he recuperates. I'm gonna go check it out."

"Oh. Okay."

The sadness that covered her face tugged at my heart. "Do you wanna go somewhere or something? Maybe to see Innvy? I can take you later."

That caused her to perk up. "Really?"

"Yeah. I'll text you when I'm wrapping things up so you can get ready."

"Okay, perfect. Thank you."

With a nod, I headed out. The sooner I got this taken care of, the better. I knew she'd still be in my life because of Bully and Innvy, but damn. Being tied to her was starting to drive me crazy. The more I was around her, the more I wanted to be around her, and I had no time for consistency.

The weekend had been eventful, surprisingly. Yesterday, Merc took me to spend some time with Innvy, which was much needed. The next morning, I spent a bit more time with Rey. He was teaching me how to play Chess while we listened to music. Under different circumstances, I would have loved to get to know the older gentleman who was becoming like a second father to me. Even with these circumstances, I was glad Rey wanted to keep me safe and that I felt so comfortable in his space.

He gave me a bit more insight into Merc, which I appreciated. He told me that, because of Merc's line of work, he was very guarded and reserved. I already felt like that was the case, but he told me the day at my store was the first day Merc had ever not been fully alert with a client. I asked what made him lose himself in that moment, and Rey told me it was a family issue that he couldn't speak on. I wondered if that family was a wife and children I didn't know about. Even with the night we'd spent together at the bar, I'd never asked Merc if he was single. Hell, it didn't matter, because I was in a relationship.

Now, I wondered if he had a family at home and if that was why he didn't spend the night with us.

Since it was Sunday, I wanted to go see my parents. Usually, I would have gone to church and brunch with them. It felt so weird not following my daily routine, but I was dedicated to staying here if it meant I would be safe.

Rey had been moving around slowly, against his doctor's orders. So when I heard him say, "You stopping by again today? Neo must be the reason," in the hallway, it made me smile.

I knew *exactly* who he was talking to.

"She's a part of it," Merc replied with that husky tone I loved to hear. "Aries and Marz went out of town. They won't be back until tonight, so I'm tryna keep myself busy too."

Aries... was that his wife?

I shouldn't have felt jealous or possessive, but I felt both.

It was silly of me to get attached to Merc.

Regardless of how much time we spent together, this was a job for him.

I was just a woman he kept safe if I left this mansion. Nothing more.

There was a light knock on the door before it slowly creaked open. Not bothering to turn and face who it was, I continued to look out of the window. Suddenly, I was less happy about Merc being here.

"You wanna get out for a while?" he asked, making his way over to me.

"You can just drop me off at my parents' house. You don't have to stay."

"I do, actually. It's my job."

With a chuckle, I bit down on my bottom lip as he sat next to me. "Yeah, I know."

His hand caressed my shoulder, and unlike usual when his touch would calm me, it irritated me. I didn't want him touching me, knowing there was a woman in his home, in his life. I shouldn't have been surprised. Merc was fine as hell. His tall, muscular frame was covered with chocolate colored skin the same as mine. He had a tapered fade and short beard that was always shiny and neatly trimmed. Tight, dark eyes and skin-colored juicy lips often fought for my attention.

Casually, I removed myself from his touch. Releasing a sigh, I stood and headed toward the closet where I'd been storing my things.

"Wassup witchu?" His tone had deepened. His expression hardened. Avoiding his eyes, I sat on the edge of the bed and put on my shoes. I was dressed casually in a form fitting cream sweatsuit, and I paired it with cream platform sandals from Tory Burch to match since it wasn't too cold outside. The weather was up and down right now, and I wanted to take full advantage of it being in the sixties.

"Nothing," I grumbled.

The chuckle he released was more irritated than amused. "If you don't want to talk about it, say that, but don't lie to me."

"Fine, I don't want to talk about it."

"Why not?" he asked, following me out of the room.

"Because it's not worth talking about."

"Anything concerning you is worth talkin' about." He gently gripped my wrist, stopping my movement. "Wassup?" he asked again, this time softer.

I wasn't sure how to even broach the subject without

sounding crazy. How was I mad that he had a woman when I had a man too? We might not have been on the best of terms, but still. I was in a relationship.

"Are you in a relationship?"

His brows wrinkled as he processed my question. They relaxed and he smiled. Releasing my wrist, Merc chuckled.

"No."

"Okay. Are you attached to a woman or having a consistent sexual relationship with her?"

His laugh was a little louder. "Neo..."

"Or a man? No judgment here."

"Aight, na. You goin' too fuckin' far."

His flaring nostrils made me smile.

"Are you?"

"No," he responded firmly. "Where is this coming from anyway?"

"I was just wondering. I'm starting to get a little attached to you, and I don't want to do that if you're in a relationship."

"I'm not in a relationship, nor am I attached to a woman or fucking one consistently. Or a man. But you shouldn't get attached to me anyway."

This time, it was him leading the way down the hall. Relief filled me, and I couldn't stop the comfortable smile that kept my lips spread as I followed him.

"Why not?" I took his hand into mine, making him chuckle and shake his head.

"I'm a gangsta, Neo. Ain't shit about my life set up for a romantic relationship. Plus, don't you have a man? Well, he ain't really a man, but that's a topic for a different conversation."

"You don't even know him."

"I know enough." His crisp tone and serious expression

made me pout and feel even more stupid because he was right. Merc had picked up on Steven's energy in one night; meanwhile, it had taken me two years. But to my credit, our relationship wasn't always like this.

I was so caught up in Steven that I almost overlooked what he called himself.

A gangster.

To me, Merc had been nothing but a gentleman.

Well, he did kill two men and wound one as if it was nothing.

If he was a gangster, a member of a criminal organization, did that mean Rey was into illegal things and that's why people were after him?

Had I been too naïve and trusting? Was what was going on more serious than I realized?

"Are you a drug dealer? Is Rey? Is that why people were shooting at him?"

Merc's grip on my hand tightened as he stroked it with his thumb. His smile was playful as he looked down at me. "Okay, detective. Don't start asking questions you don't really want or need the answer to." He paused as he opened the door to let me out then added, "Besides, on the off chance the police find Gatlin before I do, the less you know about the shooting... the better."

That was all I needed to hear. My questions stopped, and I also decided against letting him take me to my parents' house. If someone *was* watching Rey and us, I didn't want to lead them to my parents.

"Um... we don't have to go to my parents' house," I said as he opened the door of a white Challenger for me to get in.

The left side of his mouth lifted into a smirk before he licked his lips, eyeing my frame fully. "You scared now?"

"N-no, I-I..."

"It's cool, Neo. Just get in."

His head shook as he chuckled and gently guided me inside the car. My heart raced as I watched him calmly make his way around to the driver's side. The more I was around this man, the more curious I became about him. But now... I couldn't help but wonder if I needed to keep my distance and stay my ass at the house.

I WAS glad I didn't let my nerves get the best of me. Instead of going to my parents' house, I allowed Merc to kidnap me for the day. He took me shopping, then we went to a Grizzlies game with his crew, which included Bully and Innvy since they were dating and so stinking cute. My homegirl Harmony was there too, along with my boy Saint. We met within the Memphis music scene, and he was a connection for me to showcase local artists at my store for my monthly open mic night and concerts.

I could have almost cried when I saw Innvy, Harmony, and Saint. Though Merc stayed close, I pretty much spent the evening with my people. Saint assured me that nothing would happen to me while in their presence after he and I explained to Merc how we knew each other.

Also at the game was Kahlil and Honey, Hosea and Cartier, Elite and Denali, Supreme and Nicole, Tyreek and Janae, and Antonne and Haley.

Talk about big money and Black excellence.

That was my type of crowd for sure.

Now that it was over, I didn't want it to end. I gave all the ladies hugs, saving Harmony and Innvy for last.

"Is he taking care of you?" Innvy asked. "I'll tell Bully if he isn't."

With a giggle, I held my bestie even tighter. "He is... in his own way."

"Uh oh." She released me so we could face each other. "What does that mean?"

My eyes shifted toward Merc. Even though he appeared to be listening to what Bully and Saint were saying, his eyes were trained on me. It made my heart squeeze.

"He's weird. Like... he's very ni—kind. And generous. The man dropped stacks on me at the mall earlier like it was nothing, all because we had to waste time until the game started. He brought me things to occupy my time at the mansion, and you know I told you he kept me fed that weekend of the shooting when Bully told him I was working double shifts."

"All of that sounds great, Neo. What's the problem?"

"I don't think it's because he likes me." I didn't realize how crazy that sounded until I said it and we both laughed. "I think he's truly a gentleman. A class act. I don't know. I'm not used to it. Plus, he said he was a gangsta, which doesn't fit his character, but I guess it does because he protects and kills people. He doesn't flirt with me at all, and I don't think he even likes me. He might be physically attracted to me, but that's it. I don't know. I'm just having a hard time figuring him out."

"So to condense that, you like him, and you aren't sure he likes you too."

"Innvy..."

"You like that man," she said, voice lower as she grinned and gripped my arm. "And I don't blame you. Like, at all."

Unable to deny it, I covered my face as I giggled. "I

dooo," I whined before groaning and lowering my hands. "But he doesn't like me too. Plus, he has something going on at home that he's very tight lipped about. He basically told me not to get attached to him so..." With a shrug, I looked at Merc as he made his way over to us. "I guess I just have to get through this without falling for his weird ass even more."

"If he's anything like Bully, and I'm sure he is because they are friends, I bid you good luck with that. Chile, Bully got me sprung already, and I'm not ashamed to admit it."

"Admit what?" Bully asked, wrapping his arms around her and placing a series of kisses on her neck that made her melt and swoon.

I was truly happy for my friend. She deserved to be loved on properly, and I was glad Bully was doing that. He hadn't let up off her since that night at the bar. I prayed he stayed this way.

"That I really, really like you," Innvy confessed, turning in his embrace.

"Good, because I really, really like you too."

"Awww." I cooed while Merc's eyes rolled as he opened the door for me, making me laugh. "I'll talk to you later, bestie. Have fun tonight!"

"I will! I would say you have fun too but..." Her eyes shifted toward Merc as she cackled, causing Bully to pick her up and toss her over his shoulder, smacking her ass in the process.

"You wanna tell me what that was about?" Merc asked as I got into the car.

"Not at all," I replied with a laugh of my own.

The Next Morning

"Daddy!"

My heart squeezed at the sound of Marz's footsteps as he ran into the kitchen. I didn't even bother reminding him that he needed to be careful. I was just glad my little man was back home. Kneeling, I opened my arms and scooped him up.

"I missed you, little man."

"I missed you too."

"Did you have fun?" I checked, setting him on top of the counter so I could finish making his lunch.

"Yes, sir. It was a lots of fun. They have *all* the animals down there. I got to ride a horse! Mr. Omar's daddy said I can name one and make it my own if I keep coming to visit."

"That's great, son. I'm glad you had fun. Did you get to see the cows?"

"Yep! And it wasn't just on the ride like Mommy said. They had cows too. I got to milk one!"

"Oh Lord. They 'bout to turn my city boy into a country cub. You ain't gon' ever wanna be at home with all that going on."

Marz laughed. "Can you come with us next time?"

Rubbing the area between my stomach and chest, I shook my head. There wasn't too much I denied Marz of, but spending time with Omar and his family was at the top of that list.

"I'on know about all'at, but I'll take you to the drive-thru zoo or to Karrington's family's petting zoo. How does that sound?"

"Ooh, that sounds like fun! I can't wait!"

Karrington was an artist out of Memphis that had settled in Jasper Lane. His family had acres and acres of land there that they used for farming and harvesting fruits and vegetables for the community. It was their family tradition and legacy, though Karrington wasn't really about that life. He had desires to be known for his artistry, and I could respect that. One day, I hoped he had the courage to truly chase his dreams, or he would resent his family forever.

We continued to catch up, and he told me about all the people he met. He didn't want a big breakfast, so I made him a bowl of cereal and put a pack of Pop-Tart bites in his lunch box for if he got hungry before lunch. By the time I was done, Aries was hesitantly making her way inside. Things had been off between us since she told me she wanted to move with Omar and take Marz with her.

I understood Atlanta was like the Black Mecca, but that wasn't a good enough reason for her to follow behind Omar's ass with my son. I probably would have felt better about it if he came to me as a man and let me know his plans to provide for them both, but that hadn't been the case. Until we had that conversation, shit would remain off between us.

"Good morning, Merc," she spoke quietly, sitting next to Marz.

The sight of milk dripping down his chin made me smile. I was grateful to God to have had both parents in the home, in a healthy marriage, because they equipped me to be the best father I could possibly be. Even with me having the connections I did because of my career and having bodies behind me, my son never got that heartless, hardened version of me. It was easy for me to be soft with him. I took pride in making sure he learned from a young age that as a man, he was allowed to be expressive, warm, and loving. But make no mistake about it—he was learning to be just as lethal as I was too.

Already, he was efficient in boxing and two different kinds of martial arts because I got him started at the age of three. My son was going to be *nothing* to fuck with.

"Mornin'," I replied.

"I can take Marz to school this morning. I have an appointment, and it's right by his school."

My head shook as I headed toward the refrigerator. "Nah. I haven't seen him all weekend. I'll take him." She nodded, and the sad expression on her face softened me toward her. I knew she was doing what she thought was best, but I hated that she was wrong. I didn't claim to know everything, but I was a great judge of character. Something was off with Omar, and I wouldn't trust him with my son in a different state until I figured out what the hell it was. "Are you hungry?"

"Yes."

"Whatchu want?"

That caused her to perk up a little. "Your eggs, toast, and turkey bacon."

"I got you." She knew what she was doing. Aries hated eggs. I was the only person who made them in a way that she could eat. Asking me to make her eggs would stroke my ego. "Is this an appointment for..." I paused, unsure if she'd told Marz he was going to be a big brother yet. "Your stomach?"

"Yeah." Her shoulders slouched and she pouted. "And Omar can't come. It'll be the first ultrasound and I have to do it alone because he couldn't take off work."

"You want me to go with you?"

With a gasp, she stood and rushed me at the stove. Her arms wrapped around me, and I couldn't help but return the embrace.

"Please, please, please! I'll love you forever."

Chuckling, I gave her a kiss on the temple like I always did when she hugged me. "You gon' do that regardless." Her eyes rolled playfully as she released me. "We still need to talk though, Aries."

"Okay, I promise."

I was content with the temporary truce we appeared to have, so I'd let it ride for now.

NEO WAS STARING at me like she had something on her mind, but she wasn't saying shit. It was cute, like a lot of things she did. After dropping my little man off and going to Aries's appointment with her, I went to work out then showered and scooped Neo up for lunch. She said she loved fruit and seafood, so I took her to this new seafood spot that had recently opened.

We hadn't talked much, and I was intentionally limiting conversation between us. I could tell she liked me, and I didn't want her to. Because then, I'd start to like her too. Wiping my mouth, I looked over at her, and she didn't even try to hide the fact that she was staring at me. I couldn't help but laugh, which made her smile and look away.

"Some' on your mind, Neo?"

"Are all bodyguards so... brooding and quiet?"

Am I brooding? With a clipped chuckle, she rubbed between my brows, and they were scrunched. I hadn't even realized I was frowning until she did that.

"I'm not brooding... and I'm not quiet. I'm alert."

"You are brooding, and you're *always* alert. Even when we're at the house."

"My alertness keeps you safe."

"Maybe, but I don't know. I guess I just wish we could talk more. I want to know you."

Her request caught me off guard. It also flattered me. I couldn't recall the last time a woman wanted to get to know me for me and not my money, past, or reputation. Now, I was the one staring at her. She blushed and looked away.

"Why?"

"Why do I want to get to know you?" I nodded. "You're interesting. The more time we spend together, the more curious I am about you. And I know this won't last forever, but we'll be in each other's lives because of Bully and Innvy. Can we be friends?"

That was true. Once my time with her and Rey was over, we'd still be connected as long as Bully and Innvy were attached. I guess I couldn't stay completely detached from her. I didn't want to be the reason things were weird when we hung out as a crew. As much as I wanted to talk to Neo and get inside her mind and heart, I'd convinced myself it was best if we kept our distance. She reminded me too much of Aries with her romantic situation, and I couldn't allow her to be another woman I tried to save from a man who didn't deserve her.

"Yeah, I guess we can be friends."

"Yay." She clapped softly and did a little shimmy in her seat that made me blush because she was so happy to be... attached to me? *The fuck?*

"Why you so happy about being my friend?"

"I like you, duh." She said it so casually it caught me off guard. Clearing my throat, I took a sip of my water as her smile faded. "Not romantically. I mean, I like you as a friend. You're very layered, and I'm curious about you. But I don't mean I like you like you."

"Yeah, okay." Now, she was the one flustered as I relaxed into a confident state of having more of her attention than she wanted me to have. "We can get to know each other, Neo. What's the first thing you want to ask?"

"Who's waiting at home for you when you leave me?"

"My son."

We mirrored each other's smiles as she leaned closer. "There's a tiny you roaming this earth? I bet he's adorable. Tell me about him."

I did. Telling her about Marz led to me telling her about my family and upbringing. My friends. My education and career. She shared the same. We talked about our love for music and how we both paid homage to it in similar ways. I used to play for artists while she highlighted them. Some of my best memories were of me going on tour or playing in a band for singers and rappers alike. I could play drums, piano, and violin. Neo could play guitar, piano, and the harp.

We left the restaurant and went to a music store, where we played one instrument after another together. We did that shit for hours, not preparing to leave until the store was closed. I noticed the shift in her mood and figured she didn't want to go back to the mansion, so I pulled the manager aside and asked him, "How much is it going to take for you to let me and my girl stay here for another hour or so?"

He squeezed the back of his neck and checked the time on his watch. "My wife is waiting for me, big brotha."

Pulling out my wallet, I peeled off ten hundred-dollar bills. "Will this make her a little more patient?"

His eyes widened as he nodded. "It sure will. I'll be in my office. Stay for as long as you want to."

"Aight, 'preciate ya."

I made my way back over to Neo as she twirled a thick loc around her finger. In a different world, I'd have her ass barefoot and pregnant six times over. She wouldn't have a care in this world. I'd give whatever it took to make her happy. In this world, we could only be friends, and even that felt like it had a timeframe on it. Bully seemed to be serious about Innvy, but love was fickle these days. It didn't last forever the way old folks said it would.

"Well, I guess it's time for us to go, huh?" she asked, trying to mask her disappointment.

"Not just yet." Taking her by the hand, I led her over to the baby grand that she'd first fallen in love with. We sat down and I told her, "We got some more time."

With a squeal, she gave me a hug and kiss on the cheek before pulling out her phone and setting it up to record us. That wasn't usually my style, but I didn't mind the idea of her having something to remember this moment by. Maybe I'd get her to send it to me too.

"What should we play?" she asked, running her fingers across the keys and making me wish they were my skin.

"Whatever describes how you feel right now."

When she started to play a mashup of "Loved by You" by KIRBY and "Someone's Lady" by Jessie J, I liked her a little more.

Not just because of her artistry but because of the way she expressed herself. I joined in, and we continued to play until the sun came up. That was the first time I'd ever done something so intimate, and the shit felt better than sex.

Instead of taking her back to the mansion, I found myself taking her to my home, which was a first. She'd fallen asleep on the way, so I picked her up and carried her to my bedroom. I put her in the center of my bed and gave her a kiss on the forehead that caused her to gently stir, but she didn't wake up. I didn't get in with her as much as I wanted to. I crashed on the small sofa in front of the floor-to-ceiling windows and fell asleep with a smile on my face.

When I woke up, I knew immediately I wasn't at Rey's mansion. Sitting up in bed, I looked around the room. My eyes landed on Merc. His large frame was hanging off the small couch in front of large windows on the side of what I assumed was his bedroom.

It had classic bachelor vibes—large bed and TV, black and brown décor. Plants were in every corner of the room. He had the softest pillows and sheets I'd ever felt.

Getting out of bed, I checked the time on my phone that was on the nightstand next to my purse. It was just after three in the afternoon, which didn't surprise me because it was early morning when we left the music store. I couldn't remember the last time I had that much fun.

I made my way over to Merc and gave him a soft kiss on the side of his mouth. Before I could walk away, his hand grabbed my waist. His eyes slowly fluttered open and settled on me.

"Mornin'," he said, and the raspiness of his voice made my pussy throb.

"It's actually afternoon."

Shooting up, Merc cleared his throat and checked the time on his Rolex. "Shit. I did not mean to sleep that late."

"Obviously, you needed it. We both did."

With a yawn, he stood. "There are extra towels and toothbrushes and shit in the bathroom. After you freshen up, I'll take you back to the mansion."

"Okay." I agreed before heading that way.

I wasn't sure why I expected our time together to continue or at least end differently. Maybe he brought me here because it was closer than Rey's place and he was too tired to make the drive. Whatever the reason, I freshened up while he did the same in another part of his home. When we were done, he drove me back to Rey's mansion in silence. It felt like the walls he'd had up were right back up, and all the progress we made yesterday meant nothing.

I didn't have the energy to even care anymore. I couldn't force Merc to share himself with me. Though I felt like we had a lot in common and could be really good friends, if that wasn't what he wanted, it wouldn't happen. I didn't allow him to fully get the car in park good before I was opening the door to hop out. Before I could, he was gripping my arm and pulling me back inside.

"Why you in such a fuckin' rush?"

"I didn't want to hold you up more than spending yesterday with me already has."

He released a tired sigh and my arm at the same time. "Go get dressed. I planned something for you today, but I do need to go back home and spend some time with my son. I'll be back at six. And if you ever open a door while you're in the car with me, I'ma choke you with that damn seat belt."

There was no denying how serious he was by his expression, but that didn't stop the laugh that erupted from the pit of my belly. Deciding not to test his threat, I waited for him to get out and open the door for me. He didn't step back right away, which forced me to brush my body against his and step around him. I saw his eyes lower to my ass out of the corner of my eye, causing me to slow my steps and put a little extra sway in my hips. We may have agreed to be only friends, but I was for damn sure going to make him suffer for it.

MERC WAS AN ANOMALY—A gangster... a gentleman. Scary yet sweet. Brooding yet beautifully light in this hour of darkness for me. The surprise he had was a spa evening that was followed up with us going to the blues and jazz lounge that was right down the street. Bully and Beethoven happened to be there, and though we spent a little time talking with them, Merc allowed me to have him to myself.

Everything was going well until Merc spotted someone that evoked a rage in him that I didn't think I'd ever see. One minute, we were talking and vibing to the music, and the next, he was taking me over to Bully and Toe and telling them to keep me safe. His movements were careful and calculated until the man noticed him, then Merc was hopping over tables to ensure he was unable to get away. Swift punches to the man's face caused everyone around them to disperse. A gun was pulled by one of the men that was with him, and Merc effortlessly took it and pointed it at him, and it was complete chaos at that point.

While Bully carried me out, Toe charged in Merc's direction. I didn't want to leave Merc. In my mind, I knew this was literally what he got paid to do... Even if that wasn't Gatlin, it was clearly someone he had unfinished business with. In my heart, I wanted to help him. That was proven to be impossible when Bully shoved me into his SUV.

"You need to go help him!" I yelled, trying to remove myself from his grip.

"They got it. And you ain't going back in there. You'll only be in the way."

I couldn't deny that, so as much as I wanted to go back inside, I crossed my arms over my chest as my leg shook in anxiousness. "Was that Gatlin?"

"No, but it was someone connected to him."

Relief filled me. Hopefully, the man would be able to lead Merc to Gatlin so this would all be over. Bully's phone began to ring, and Merc's name was on the dashboard.

"Yeah?" Bully answered.

"Take her to Rey. I'll be there later."

"Aight, gotchu."

The ride to Rey's place was done in silence on my part. Bully tried to keep my mind off things by talking about nothing in particular, and I appreciated the distraction, but it was hard for me to focus. I wouldn't be able to be at peace until I was sure Merc was going to make it out of this okay.

When we got to the mansion, Rey made sure I was okay before assuring me Merc knew exactly what he was doing and would be fine. I went to the room I'd been occupying and almost crumbled when I saw one of the keyboard's Merc and I had been playing yesterday in the corner of the room. It had a red bow on it and a small card that read:

Hopefully this will help you pass the time and make some beautiful music in the process.
– Merc

Holding the card to my chest, I closed my eyes and said a silent prayer for both his and Beethoven's safety... and for him to come back to me soon.

THE FEEL of an arm wrapping around me caused my eyes to pop open. Turning in bed, I gasped at the sight of Merc. Pulling him down to me, I surprised myself by kissing his lips. I pulled away quickly to apologize, but his lips on mine silenced me. Quick pecks turned into his tongue sliding into my mouth as I tugged him further into the bed. He released a low moan against my lips that made my nipples harden.

When he was in bed completely, I wrapped my arms and legs around him.

As much as I enjoyed kissing him, I pulled away to say, "I was so scared."

"I told you I wasn't going to let anything happen to you," he reminded.

"I know that. I was scared for *you*. If anything would have happened to you because of me..." My eyes watered and head shook at the thought. "I don't want you doing this for me anymore. It was different before I knew you had a son."

Merc smiled softly as he pushed my locs out of my face. He kissed my forehead, each eye, my nose, then my lips.

"This is what I wanted to avoid, Neo."

His voice was low, tone calm and even.

"Some things can't be avoided, Mercury. And me liking and caring about you is one."

He returned his lips to mine briefly before pulling away and getting out of the bed. "We don't need to be doin' this. You in a whole relationship, and I've never been a cheater. I don't intend to be the man you cheat with either."

Shit.

I'd forgotten all about Steven.

Running my fingers through my locs, I swallowed hard.

"I'm not a cheater either. I... just got caught up in the moment. It won't happen again."

With a nod, he took a step back from the bed. "I just wanted to let you know I was good. Bully said you were worried."

Avoiding his eyes, I clenched the sheets and nodded. "Gatlin?"

"We have his cousin. We're using him as bait. He'll pop out soon."

"Okay. Thanks."

He left, and it wasn't until I was alone that I felt like I could breathe again. Cursing under my breath, I held back tears. I couldn't believe I'd kissed him. I had never done something like that before in my life. Even with the issues Steven and I were having, he didn't deserve that. I'd have to go see him and try to figure out where we going to go from here. With the history we had, our chemistry had been dull lately. Add to that the lack of effort and I was finally ready to end our relationship.

My thoughts were all over the place, and when I realized I wouldn't be getting to sleep anytime soon, I started to scroll on social media. I got on my store's TikTok page to add a few clips of me and Merc playing at the store. It took a little effort, but I was able to blur his face out before uploading the clips. While I didn't care about people knowing we knew each other, until I talked to Steven, I didn't feel comfortable showcasing another man on my page, even if it was for creative content.

As I scrolled the For You Page, my heart immediately dropped when a video of Steven, Asia, and China came up. I took note of the name because, as far as I knew, neither of them had a TikTok page. I could tell by the decorations that it was for Valentine's Day, so I clicked on the video. The caption was:

When your baby daddy makes Valentine's Day special for you and his daughter.

They were at Asia's home, and it was decorated with banners, streamers, roses, and balloons. She recorded Steven gifting them both several gifts before the clip changed and showed them at a restaurant. After dinner, another clip showed them on a horse and carriage ride. It ended with Steven kissing China goodnight and tucking her in bed, then Asia told him to tuck her in bed. The last clip was of them in her bed and his hand sliding up her naked leg.

My eyes blurred as I went from one video to another. She had several of them together. Almost every time he told me he was going to spend time with China, he was spending time with Asia too. I couldn't understand for the life of me why none of these videos had come up before. Noticing the location, Asia put her neighborhood specifically, so that could have been why. If she was close to Rey, that was why she was on my feed. It didn't explain why she wasn't coming up on my personal page.

I switched accounts, and my intuition told me to go and

look at the pages that had been blocked on my account. Scoffing, I hopped out of bed when I noticed her page had been blocked and his. I wasn't sure when Steven had done that, but it made me question if he'd done it on my other social media pages too. It didn't matter at this point. I'd seen all I needed to see. This man was in a damn relationship with his baby mama. The baby mama he swore nothing was going on with. This was exactly why I never wanted to deal with a man who had children, but Steven swore he was different and that things between him and Asia didn't go beyond their child.

How could I have been so fucking *stupid*?

After reserving an Uber, I tossed on a hoodie and some sweatpants, determined to go *see* Steven. He was going to have to make this shit make sense because I couldn't understand what could possibly make him think it was okay to play in my face like this.

As soon as the Uber arrived, I dotted out of the house, ignoring Rey calling my name.

A part of me wanted to call Steven, but the other part of me told me to pull up. I didn't want him to get a hint that something was wrong because of my tone, and there was no way I'd be able to fake the funk with him right now.

When I arrived, I asked the Uber driver to wait for me. I didn't know Rey's address, so it would be easier to have him to just take me back. I let myself inside of the home I shared with Steven, and immediately, the sound of Asia's laughter filled my ears. My anger only intensified at the thought of him playing house with them while I was away for my safety. No wonder he hadn't been calling and texting to make sure I was good. He was taking full advantage of my absence by having his baby mama here.

I found them in the living room cuddled up, watching a movie. At the sight of me, Steven quickly pushed Asia off him and stood.

"Neo... Bae... hey. What are you doing here?"

I had all these words I wanted to say, but seeing them together left me speechless. Before I could stop myself, I was punching Steven in his nose.

"How could you!" I yelled as my eyes watered, but not from sadness... from anger. "Not only do you cheat on me, but you do it with *this* bitch? If you wanted to be a family with her, why didn't you just say that shit? You know how many niggas have tried to get at me that I rejected to be faithful to your ass, and you do this to me?"

While one hand covered his bleeding nose, the other grabbed my wrist and pulled me into his chest.

"Did you just fucking hit me?"

"You didn't feel it? Maybe I need to do it again."

Before I could smack him, Steven picked me up and started carrying me out of the living room, but the sound of the door behind kicked in caused him to set me down on my feet. At the sight of a limping man pointing a gun in our direction, my heart stopped beating.

Gatlin.

He'd been watching Rey's home... waiting... and my ass had led him right to my home without Merc being here to protect me.

"I promise I won't tell the police you shot Rey," I told him, voice trembling as I lifted my shaking hands in surrender.

"You think I trust you?" Gatlin asked, taking a step in my direction. "No witnesses."

My eyes closed as I pulled in a deep breath.

"Let's talk about this," Steven said, pulling me behind him.

I was surprised he was even trying to help me. It didn't make me hate him even less. Nothing would be able to take away the anger and hurt over him cheating on me with his baby mama, not even him getting Gatlin to spare my life...

Anything between us was forbidden. Keeping Neo safe was my job. A job I took seriously and couldn't allow lustful desires to cloud. Even with that logic swirling around in my mind, feelings for Neo planted themselves deeper and deeper in the center of my heart. It was taking everything inside of me not to tell her to break up with her nigga so she could know how it felt to be loved by a real one. I was truly at war with myself as I drove back home.

An incoming call pulled me out of my thoughts. At the sight of Rey's number, I accepted the call and allowed it to connect to the Bluetooth in my car.

"You good?" I checked.

"I am, but Neo's not." Immediately, I made a U-turn and headed back in the direction of his mansion.

"What's going on?"

"She took an Uber and left. Trent was at the door, and he said she was mumbling about her man playing in her face and how he had her fucked up. So I assume she's going wherever he is."

"Aight, let me get off the phone so I can track her down."

Without waiting for him to agree, I ended the call. I figured she was going back home, but I checked her location to be sure. Sure enough, that's where it looked like she was going.

What had he done to make her not only leave but leave without me?

That didn't matter right now.

I just needed to get to her and make sure she was safe.

Now that we had Chico in our possession, Gatlin was going to show up sooner or later. I didn't want her being in her feelings to lead her into a trap that he'd set up for her and to get his cousin back.

I didn't think Neo realized just how serious this was, and maybe that was my and Rey's fault. In our attempt to shield her from everything that was going on, neither of us told her that he was the head over a multi-million-dollar drug empire that his best friend and business partner was trying to get him out of.

It took me about thirteen minutes to get to Neo's place, and as soon as I turned onto the street, I saw someone with a limp crossing her lawn. Accelerating my speed, I pulled my Glock from underneath the seat. By the time I crept into the house, Gatlin was saying, "No witnesses."

"Let's talk about this," a man that I assumed to be Steven said, pulling Neo behind him.

Her eyes closed and body shook.

"Ain't shit to talk about," Gatlin said.

"You right about that." At the sound of my voice, Gatlin

turned, and I sent three bullets into his chest. I walked over to him and put two more into his skull for good measure.

The screams of a woman on the couch didn't faze me. Steven shielded Neo, but she pushed him off her as she yelled, "Get off me! I hate you! I can't believe you would do this to me!"

Steven scoffed as I sent Bully a numbered code via text, requesting a cleanup crew.

"This man just killed someone in front of us, and you're standing up here yelling about me cheating?"

"You cheated on her?" I asked before chuckling. "Fuckin' fool."

"I need to get the hell up out of here!" ol' girl yelled as she tried to make a run for it, but I grabbed her and pushed her toward Steven.

"Neither one of y'all are going anywhere. Not yet anyway."

My eyes shifted in Neo's direction, and she was shaking in anger. I didn't see an ounce of sadness in her face or eyes; this was all rage. The dried-up blood on Steven's nose and lips I assumed was her doing. I needed her to focus, so I pulled her to my side.

"I have a cleanup crew coming, but I have to finish this tonight. You need to go back to Rey's until I do." When her eyes went back to them, I gripped her chin and forced her to look at me. "Whatever you got going on with him don't matter right now. Focus on me." Her eyes closed, and she inhaled a deep breath. With a nod, she gave me her eyes. "If I don't get rid of Bart tonight, this shit is going to be even worse. Bully is going to stay with you and Rey until this is over."

"What about you? Who's going with you?"

Her concern made me smile. "I'll pick up Toe, but please, don't worry about me. I'll be good."

Tears filled her eyes as they fluttered. With a nod, she wrapped her arms around me. I hugged her back before placing a kiss to her forehead. After telling Steven and ol' girl to sit down and not make a move, I went outside to see if her Uber driver had left. I wasn't worried about her neighbors hearing the shooting, because I'd used a silencer. Since he was still here, I sent her back with him and told her to text me when she made it back to Rey. We hugged again, and I watched her go to the car in case Gatlin had come with someone who was waiting outside.

I made my way back to Gatlin's lifeless body and used his thumb to open his phone. After sending his father a text, letting him know I had Neo, I waited for his response. Like I figured he would, Bart told him to bring her to him. Since I didn't know where he was, I checked his contact information and hoped they shared their locations. Thankfully, they did.

Once Bully and the cleanup crew pulled up, I let Beethoven know I was on my way to him.

I didn't think Steven would snitch, knowing this man was going to kill Neo, but just to be safe, Bully had been given the pleasurable task of making sure they understood what would happen if word about what happened here spread. There was no doubt in my mind that the promise of them having the same fate as Gatlin would keep them quiet. And if it didn't, I'd gladly put a bullet between Steven's bitch ass eyes just because he broke Neo's heart.

Two Weeks Later

"You don't have to be in a rush to leave," Rey said as I put my bags in the back of the town car he requested to take me home.

The night Gatlin was killed and I became aware of Steven's cheating, Merc handled Bart. I wasn't sure what exactly happened, but the following day, news of his and Gatlin's disappearance had made the news. When Merc came to let Rey know the job was completed, he quit and left soon after I thanked him for yet again saving my life.

Even though I could have gone home, I stayed with Rey. It was crazy how I'd gone from being anxious to return to my normal life to wanting to avoid it because of Steven's infidelity. Here I was feeling consumed by guilt over a kiss, while he'd been carrying on a relationship for God only knows how long with his baby mama. I didn't even have the stomach to go through their profiles to put together a timeframe based on their videos.

When Rey heard about what happened, he told me I didn't have to be in a rush to leave, which I appreciated. It made me smile knowing that two weeks later, he shared the same sentiment. I'd meant it when I said he was becoming like a second father to me, but it was time for me to stop running from my failed relationship and get back to my life.

"I'll be back to visit."

"You promise?"

"Of course. I'm going to keep my keyboard here, so that way you know I'll be back."

He gave me a warm hug and stuffed something in my bag, telling me, "Don't let anything he says keep you in that house. Leave, Neo, no matter what."

"I will." I assured him with a nod.

We embraced again before I got in the town car. I checked my bag, and a smile lifted the corners of my lips when I saw the stacks of money he put inside. I sent my parents a text in our group chat, letting them know I was finally on my way back home, and they reminded me that I could come there as soon as I was done packing a few things. Daddy had already told me he had a moving company on standby to take my things to storage when I was ready. I didn't feel any tugs in my heart that wanted to stay with Steven and try and work things out.

Even before I saw the videos, I'd kind of made up in my mind to end things. Finding out that he was cheating only solidified I was making the right decision to remove him from my life.

I had purposefully chosen a weekday afternoon to go and grab a few things plus my car, so I was surprised when

I went inside and found him in the bedroom. He immediately leaped from bed and started toward me, but I lifted my hands to stop him.

"I've been waiting for you to come home," he said. "There's a lot we need to discuss."

"No there's not, actually. You cheated and we're over."

As I headed to the closet, he followed me. "I know that might have looked bad, but Asia was just keeping me company while you were gone. That's it."

Laughing, I pulled my rolling luggage out of the closet and placed it on the bed.

"You're lying."

"Bae, I'm telling you the truth." Steven grabbed my hand. "There was nothing going on between me and Asia before you left."

I hadn't told him about me seeing her TikTok, so I could understand why he thought he could get away with lying. The crazy thing was, I didn't even have the energy to go back and forth with him. I didn't have the energy to watch him scramble and try and finesse the truth.

"Steve, it's clear you are attached to that woman. Be with her and leave me the hell alone."

For a while, he just stood there and stared at me. I couldn't believe I didn't see the signs. How he randomly stopped bringing China here and opted to spend time with her outside of the house. How he somehow grew busier at work but never seemed to make more money. How we stopped having sex and going out and he was totally okay with it.

"So you're just going to leave me? You're not even going to try and work this out?" he asked as I started to gather things from the bathroom.

God. I hated I'd even moved in with him. We'd been

staying together for the last year. It happened right after he gifted me with the building for my store. It was crazy because he'd been acting suspicious and secretive, and I thought it was because he was about to propose. The building was even better. I was so grateful I agreed to move in with him, even though I'd been against it for a while.

The more I thought about it, the more it made sense. That was when he started acting sketchy and staying out more. That was also when Asia started getting real cocky and limiting the time China could be with us here. Now I couldn't help but wonder if Steven gifted me with the store because of guilt or as a way to keep me with him if and when I found out about his cheating.

When I ignored him, he continued. "Fine. If you don't want me, then you don't want nothing that I gave you. So I hope you're ready to pack all your shit tonight, because you can't come back after this."

Amusement filled me as I tossed my things into my bag. "Okay, that's fine, Steve."

"And the music store too."

Now that made me pause and finally give him the attention he wanted. "What?"

"That's in my name. I leased that building for you. So if you don't want me, you don't want the store either."

I stared at him as confusion filled me. I couldn't believe he was serious. With a chuckle, I placed my hand on my hip. "You don't know shit about running a vinyl music store. What reason would you have to keep it other than to hurt me?"

"That's more than enough for me."

My smile fell as I pulled in a deep breath. "So let me get this straight." Putting my hands in prayer position, I looked toward the ceiling. "You cheat on me, and when I find out and leave you, you decide to force me to stay with you or lose the thing I love the most?"

He took slow steps in my direction. "That's exactly what I'm saying." Steven was so confident I would agree that he began to take my clothing out of my bag. "I can fix this if you give me a chance. You've worked hard to turn that store into what it is. I know you're not going to be dumb enough to give that up just because I made a mistake."

"That's where you're wrong, Steven." I snatched my clothes out of his arms. "I won't be bullied into staying with you. So if you want to cause me even more pain by taking my store away from me, fine. I'll rebuild without you."

With a shrug, he walked away. I said I wouldn't cry in front of this man, so I was glad he left. I was cool with leaving our home. What I wasn't prepared for was for him to take my store from me. Even though the business was mine, the building was in his name. Since he was paying to own it, if he wanted me out, I had no choice but to leave.

I jogged into the bathroom and slammed the door behind me as my tears started to pour. Sliding down it, I asked God why this was happening to me. It was one thing for me to lose the man I loved and thought I'd be with forever, but now, I was losing my passion and joy too. When I was composed enough, I asked my parents and Innvy to come help me pack. The sooner I got away from this man... the better.

I LOVED MY PEOPLE.

As soon as my parents arrived, my mood was lifted.

They'd brought several of my cousins and aunts and uncles along too.

What started as them helping me pack my things turned into a moving out party. We were well into the night, drinking, dancing, and enjoying ourselves. Steven left quickly when my cousins arrived because he didn't want no smoke, and all I could do was laugh.

I gave him the courtesy of letting him know when I was leaving, and I also cleaned up, though a part of me wanted to leave the house a mess since he wanted to be so damn messy.

As I headed out to the garage to get in my car, he was pulling up with China and Asia in his. Asia couldn't wait to get out and taunt me with, "I'm glad your ass is finally gone so I can come back to where I rightfully belong."

Under normal circumstances, I would never fight over a man, but when I punched her silly ass, it had nothing to do with Steven and everything to do with the way she'd been disrespecting me. Innvy came rushing into the garage as China screamed for her mama, daring Asia to get up and try to swing back.

I told her crazy ass to go back to her car and let me know when she made it home. My parents wanted me to trail them to their place, but I wasn't ready to settle down just yet. Even though the random party had briefly put me in good spirits, the weight of my reality hit my heart as I pulled out of the garage and driveway.

My relationship was over, my store was taken from me, and I had nothing to call my own other than my car. Figuring a drive would help me ease my mind, I told my parents I'd let them know when I was on my way to their place so they wouldn't be startled by my late arrival. Daddy asked me if I was sure because it was supposed to start snowing soon, but I didn't care. It didn't snow too bad in Memphis anyway, so I was sure I would be fine.

So maybe leaving in the middle of the night wasn't the *best* idea. It wasn't my intention. Had I known Steven would give me an ultimatum—accept his bullshit or give up my home, business, and the life we were building—I would have been more prepared to make my escape. No part of my mind or heart wanted to believe the man I'd spent the last two years with could be so heartless and selfish. He knew how much music and my vinyl store meant to me. That was why he'd given it to me for our anniversary one year ago. I preferred it over an engagement ring, and now, I had neither.

It didn't matter how much I told myself it was better I get away from Steven now after seeing the real him—my heart still hurt over how the man I loved could treat me this way. It also didn't help that I had "Nothing But Love" by Lu Kala on repeat. Tears blurred my eyes as I belted the lyrics. It was as if she'd written the song just for me.

I had no real destination in mind as I drove. I could have gone to a friend's house or to my parents' home, but I didn't want to talk about what was going on with me and Steven. Under normal circumstances, I wouldn't be driving in the dark or while it was snowing.

The further I got into my drive, the worse the snow got. I'd filled up my tank before hopping on the interstate, and though I didn't check the time I started driving, since I would soon be out of gas, I assumed I'd been on the road for at least five or six hours. Unintentionally, it seemed I'd taken a familiar trail to a mountain town like Gatlinburg from my home in Memphis. Because of how windy it was and how heavy the snow was falling, I didn't want to risk driving through the mountains.

My decision not to continue driving was finalized when I got stuck in a snowdrift. I didn't think anything could make my night or my life worse, but here I was, stuck in the middle of nowhere in a huge pile of snow. Curses and cries left me as I yelled and punched the steering wheel. I was mad at Steven for betraying and abandoning me. I was mad at God for making this godforsaken snow. I was mad at myself for not paying attention to where I was driving and ending up in a snowy town so late at night.

Checking the time, I sighed at the sight of 10:39 p.m. Wiping my face, I inhaled what I hoped would be a calming breath. I tried to request a tow truck, but my insurance company's app didn't work. My outgoing calls weren't working either. If the sun was out, I'd sit in my car and hope help would drive by. Because it was pitch black out, I didn't want to risk a car coming and hitting me.

So, I got out and grabbed the two bags I packed in my car before leaving and headed north. I couldn't remember the last house I'd passed, and there were only two lights shining ahead. I had no idea what I was walking into, but anything at this point would have been better than being stuck with no service in the cold. As I headed toward the lights, I prayed they wouldn't lead to a serial killer who planned to make me their next victim.

The world must be ending, just like mine. It was the first day of spring, yet there was a snowstorm happening. I checked the time on my phone when I thought I heard knocking. That couldn't have been the case. Not only because it was so late at night but also because my cabin in Massie Manor was miles away from anything and anyone. I'd specifically purchased this cabin because it was secluded. Regardless of the season, this was where I came when I had a lot on my mind and needed time away to figure things out.

This time around, the biggest thing on my mind was my son. Aries was dead set on moving to Atlanta with Omar, and outside of crippling him, there seemed like it was nothing I could do stop it. We finally sat down and talked two days ago because they wanted to take Marz back to Mississippi. I was cool with that because it was the weekend before his spring break. I didn't know it was going to be snowing in Memphis, but it worked out because I planned to take him to Orlando anyway.

They used the horses and cows to bait my little man into spending his spring break in Mississippi of all places. Even though I didn't want to be away from him for an entire week, I agreed in hopes to get things back to normal between me and Aries. But the conversation we had before they left changed all that.

"Aries said you have some reservations about them coming to Atlanta with me," Omar said, getting comfortable in the chair on the opposite end of my desk like he'd be around for long.

"Yeah, I do. First of all, you didn't approach me and ask me like a man. Second, I don't know what you plan to do for money while you're there. You're asking me to let you be a primary guardian for my son in my absence, yet I know nothing about your intentions or the move."

"Look, I'ma be honest wit' ya. I don't mind Marz staying here with you, but Aries insists on him coming with us."

Chuckling, I sat back in my seat. Rolling my tongue over my cheek, I had to keep myself from telling him to get the fuck out. That alone was reason for me to not let Marz go. If he had truly bonded with my little man and wanted him to come along, his attitude would have been different. From the sound of it, Marz was an inconvenience instead of an added gift that came from loving his mother.

"You do know that's her son, right? Of course she's going to want him to go with her."

His eyes squeezed shut as he sighed. "I didn't mean it like that. I just mean Marz is stable here, and it don't make sense for us to uproot him and take him there."

Even though I agreed, I wanted to see where his head was at, so I continued.

"You don't think the environment you provide there will be stable?"

"Not as stable as I want it to be in the beginning." Sitting

back in his seat, he crossed his arms over his chest as he grinned. "I'm going there to pursue my rap career. I got enough money saved for bills for a year. After that, it'll have to be up with my music 'cause I ain't gettin' a regular job. So I'm thinkin' if he stays here, Aries can travel with me when I need her to. We gon' have a lot of late nights and early mornings, you feel me?"

Clearing my throat didn't hide my chuckle. Some men were merely little boys in grown up bodies. There was no way this nigga was sitting here saying he was going to start a rap career at his big ass age of thirty-five with a wife, stepson, and baby on the way. I wasn't saying it wasn't possible, but the man had never mentioned wanting to rap before. He probably wasn't even any good.

Squeezing the bridge of my nose, I pulled my smirk in.

"I don't see how Aries will be able to be on the road with you. She's pregnant, Omar. And y'all about to get married. Have you factored in the costs of the wedding? It sounds like you putting a lot on your plate with this move."

"Man, say, just being honest... if I could do this shit alone, I would. But she ended up pregnant, and I'm tryna do the right thing. Plus, I really do love 'er. It's just the timing of it all."

"I'ma be honest with you. This conversation ain't making me want to allow Marz to go with you. You're right—he has a very stable life here. I'm not about to let y'all uproot him from that so you can pursue a rap career."

"And I'm cool with that," he stressed. "He can stay here. Just convince ya baby mama of that."

That shit was easier said than done.

Aries refused to leave Marz here, and he refused to leave her here. So his tune completely switched up by the time they left, and he was all for Marz going with them. At that point, I straight up told Aries that wasn't going to happen, and she did some shit I thought she'd never do—she threatened to try and get full custody so I wouldn't be able to stop her from taking my son.

That shit broke my heart.

As close as we'd been and as well as we'd been coparenting, I never thought we'd come to this. True enough, since I was the one financially taking care of her and Marz, a part of me was cool with her taking that chance. However, most judges in Memphis favored the mother whether she was paying the bills or not. I wasn't sure if I wanted to risk going to court and losing, allowing her to take my son away.

So here I was, trying to figure out how to make this shit work in a way that would be best for Marz. His mother was so blinded by her love for and loyalty to Omar that she couldn't see how dangerous of a game she was playing, following him. If she didn't have no kids and she wanted to go with him so he could chase his dreams, I'd be cool with that, but he needed more stability than a dream to care for my son and the baby she was pregnant with.

Just thinking about it caused my head to start pounding. Lying back down, I pulled in a deep breath and tried to clear my mind. Before I left this cabin, I needed God to deposit something into my mind and heart to work this out in my little man's favor. I couldn't see my life without him. Marz was the reason I'd calmed down as much as I had. He was my whole heart and soul, and I genuinely loved being his dad daily.

If I didn't see him every day, I wouldn't know what to do with myself. My life would have a huge void that nothing would be able to fill. And if anything happened to him while he was in their care...

The sound of knocking sounded off again. This time, I couldn't ignore it. Standing, I grabbed my robe off the back of the door and headed down the hall. When I opened the door, the sight of a shivering Neo surprised me. At the sight of me, she burst into tears.

I wasted no time pulling her into my arms and closing the door behind her. It was snowing even harder now, and it looked like there was at least six or seven inches of snow on the ground.

"What's wrong, baby?"

"Everything." She sobbed, holding me tighter. "I'm just glad you're here. I couldn't see any more, so I had to leave my car. I didn't know if anyone was even here, but I had to try. My phone isn't working, and I have no idea where I even am."

"Neo..." I carried her into the master bedroom and grabbed a few blankets from the closet. I put one on the floor and wrapped the other two around us with her in my lap. In front of the roaring fire, I rubbed her cold, shivering body until she began to warm up. Her cries turned into sniffles, then they eventually stopped. When they did, I asked her, "What happened?"

"Long story short, I went to get some of my things from the house today, and when Steven realized I wasn't going to take him back, he told me I had to take everything today, and he's taking my store from me."

Her eyes watered and head hung, and I instantly went into protector mode.

"The business is in his name?"

"No, but the building is. I can keep it and open it somewhere else, but I have to leave the building." With a chuckle, she wiped a tear and sniffled. "While my family was partying and helping me pack, he was at the store, apparently. After I left the house, he sent me pictures of practically all my inventory being broken." She sucked her teeth and looked toward the ceiling before swallowing back her tears. "All those vinyl records just... gone. So many classics. So many albums I'll never be able to purchase again. I can't believe he could be so spiteful and cruel. That store meant everything to me, and now I don't have anything."

"You got me," I assured her before placing a kiss on the corner of her mouth.

She smiled. "No I don't. You've made it clear there can be nothing between us, which is fine anyway. After Steven, I'm never being with a man that has kids again."

I wanted to tell her she was beginning to feel like an answer to a prayer I was too afraid to utter. The more I tried to avoid her, the more God put her in my life. Now that I was finally starting to accept that, it was Neo who was pulling away.

"Never?"

Her head shook as she pouted. "Ever."

Accepting that, even though I hated it, I told her, "I'm sorry about your store. If there's anything I can do to rectify this for you, I will."

I already had two options in mind—getting my homies to beat his ass or having my connect at MPD arrest him and his baby mama for vandalism. How Neo wanted to handle this would determine which way I'd go.

She wrapped her arms around my neck and rested her head on mine. "What're you doing here anyway?"

"Needed some time to think."

"Oh. I'm always in your way. I'll stay away until the snow clears. You won't even know I'm here."

Before she could get up from my lap, I pulled her back down. "I mean... I can't seem to get away from you, but I'm starting to like it."

Neo smiled, and I was glad. "I don't know why you want to anyway."

"I'm not fighting it anymore, for what it's worth."

Our eyes remained locked until mine lowered to her lips. I licked mine.

"Um... well... it doesn't matter anymore."

She tried to stand again. This time, I let her. Neo could run if she wanted to. If God told me what I was starting to believe in my heart—that she was mine—I'd chase her. But I wouldn't just chase her; I'd capture her and pursue her every day that I had her, to make sure she never regretted being mine.

"You want that nigga to be arrested?" I asked. "Or do you want me to send them boys to beat his ass?"

Her eyes widened, and she gasped before releasing a choked chuckle. "Uh... those are real options?"

"Hell yeah." I stood. "Which one you want?"

"Hmm..." Her mouth twisted to the side as she considered my options. "How likely is it they'll have to do time?"

"Honestly, not likely. Since it's a vandalism charge, if they don't have a record, they'll probably get probation and a fine."

Neo nodded. "Well, I don't want him to lose his job because of a charge, but I do want him to be punished. I also don't condone violence bu—"

Scoffing, I closed the space between us. "Did you forget you tried to break that mane nose?"

Her huff was cute as she crossed her arms over her chest. She had a quick temper, apparently, but she calmed down quickly, which was good.

"That wasn't one of my best moments," she muttered.

"Mhm." Chuckling, I lowered her arms from her chest. "He deserved that and a lot more. If you don't want me to get his ass beat, I'll show him how it feels for what he loves to be destroyed. Either way, he wronged you, and he gon' pay."

She nodded. "I don't want to know what you do so I won't feel guilty for it."

"Aight, say less."

She looked around the room. "Where can I sleep?" she asked.

"In here."

"Okay. Will you be close?"

Chuckling, I nodded as we began to fold the blankets. "As close as your skin."

Realization covered her face before she covered it and released a soft snicker. After I put the blankets up, I took my robe off and got back in bed. She was slow making her way over to the bed, but Neo came eventually. When she began to remove her clothing, I turned toward the wall. Once she got in bed, she made her way to the middle of it.

I turned and took her into my arms, placing her on my chest. She felt good as hell there. Like she belonged.

We both released content sighs as Neo snuggled against me. I stroked her back with one hand and her scalp with the other.

"Mercury?" she called quietly.

"Yeah?"

Instead of speaking, she kissed the center of my chest, and that was enough.

I thought I dreamed what happened last night. That maybe I fell asleep in my car and dreamed about Merc. When I woke up in this strange room, I realized that wasn't the case. My bags were on and near the rocking chair to the left of the bed, which told me he'd gone to my car. Had he been able to drive it down?

Getting out of bed, I looked out of the window and gasped. I'd never seen so much snow in my life. It had to be about twenty inches. Looking around the room, I walked over to the fireplace. Just those brief seconds by the window had sent a chill through me. Once I was warm, I grabbed the things I needed to shower and went into the bathroom, grateful I'd put the bags with my necessities in my car instead of sending them to my parents' home.

After my shower, I familiarized myself with the cabin. Its design was standard for a cabin—wood everything with burgundy and green accents. I loved that each room had a fireplace, and Merc had them all blasting, thankfully. It didn't surprise me to find him in the kitchen fixing breakfast. He was shirtless in loose fitting pajama bottoms and house shoes, looking like my favorite piece of chocolate candy.

"Good morning," I greeted, getting comfortable at the island in the center of the kitchen.

"Mornin'. How'd you sleep?"

"All things considered... great."

I figured that had to do with him, but I wouldn't admit to that.

"Thank you for going and getting my things out of the car. Were you able to drive it here?"

"Nah, it's snowed in. I was only able to get through the back door, but I could barely get through that because it was snowing so bad. I went three hours ago, and another five inches of snow have come down since then."

"Damn. Well, it looks like we'll be stuck here for a while."

"Looks that way."

If I was crazy, I'd say there was a smile on his face. "Is there anything I can do to help?"

"Nah, I got it. Thankfully, I stocked the kitchen when I arrived, so we'll be good while we're here."

"Good."

I decided to check in with my people to let them know I was good. Even though he said he didn't need me to do anything, I wanted to keep busy. When I got home, I didn't know what the hell I was going to do. Even if I reopened my store, I wouldn't have that much inventory because Steven's bitch ass had destroyed so much of my shit. I didn't even want to think about it because it would make me mad all over again. His little stunt at the store explained why they had those cocky expressions when they came back to the house last night.

While he finished up breakfast, I made us some mimosas. We ate breakfast together before playing Chess. He wanted to see how much I'd learned from Rey. I lost, but I did a hell of a lot better than I thought I would. After that, we worked out and decided to chill in bed since we were snowed in.

"Everything okay with Marz?" I asked as he searched for something to watch on Hulu.

"He's good. It's his damn mama that's driving me crazy."

"You want to elaborate on that?"

He released a sigh and put the TV on *Living Single*, though neither of us paid it any attention as he talked. By the time he was done telling me about the situation, I was speechless. I could understand why he didn't want them to take Marz and hoped he'd be able to figure something out. After expressing that, I told him if there was anything I could do to help, even if that was just by taking his mind off things, to let me know. Here I was sad over what Steven had done, and Merc was worrying about losing his son.

Silence found us, and I figured it was because he was trapped in his thoughts like we were trapped in this cabin. Well, like I was trapped in this cabin. This was exactly where he wanted to be.

"You okay?" I asked, taking his hand into mine.

Merc gave me a sad smile. "I will be."

"I'm really sorry you're going through this."

"I'm not giving him up without a fight. I'm not sure why she's even taking it here as if she doesn't know what I'm capable of. She's out her fucking mind if she thinks I'm going to let her take him from me."

"I don't know her, but I don't think it will come to that. Something in my gut is telling me God is gonna turn this situation around for all of you. Just trust Him, and for once, let Him work on your behalf." He looked away, and I gently pulled his attention back to me with my hand under his chin. "You're always there for everyone else. Let Him be here for you."

I wasn't sure which one of us moved first, but our lips connected for a deep, slow, nasty kiss. This man had the ability to unnerve me—effortlessly. His hand wrapped around my neck, and I whimpered as he gripped it while looking into my eyes. Merc released a low, cocky chuckle with a shake of his head.

"You ain't ready," he decided, releasing me.

"Yes, I am," I appealed, lowering myself further into the bed.

Spreading my legs, I allowed his shirt to slide down my thighs and puddle at my waist.

"Mm... your thighs are so fucking *sexy*."

Instead of keeping them bent as I circled my clit, Merc straightened them and began to place kisses up and down the right one. My back arched as he neared my inner thighs. His hand slid up my stomach, massaging and pinching each nipple. My breathing grew ragged as I slipped a finger into my pussy. Tugging my bottom lip into my mouth, I squirmed as his hand returned to my neck.

Merc swatted my hand away and positioned himself at my opening. The first time a man's head was between my legs was my freshman year of college. Since then, no man had ever made me cum from his mouth. It was usually a quick act of foreplay they did until my pussy was wet enough for them to enter me.

That wasn't the case with Merc.

He took his time as he feasted on my pussy. It actually caught me off guard how good it felt. When I tried to shift my body to lessen the feel of his tongue on my clit, he gripped my thighs and kept me in place.

One orgasm led to another, and he was still licking and sucking and kissing every inch of my pussy.

"Mercury," I moaned, gripping his head as he slipped two fingers inside of my opening.

Maybe I wasn't ready.

"Baby," I pleaded, toes curling as my spine tingled.

"Hmm?"

The way he looked into my eyes... as if he wasn't ripping my soul apart in the best way...

"Merc, I... I'm about to cum again."

He kept his same pace, licking a spot under the hood of my clit that I didn't even know would make me cum. Flattening his tongue, Merc touched every nerve ending in my clit, locking my body and pulling a third climax out of me like it was nothing.

"Mm... fuck!" My legs wrapped around him as I trembled. He didn't seem to care about me smothering him. In fact, he gripped my thighs tighter and continued to lick and suck until I pushed him away. "Shit. I *wasn't* ready."

His laughter made me chuckle as I took in short, choppy breaths. Merc placed a kiss to my thigh before using it to pull me back to the center of the bed.

"It's too late now. You got my shit hard as fuck, and you gon' take every drop of my cum."

"Mercury..."

Pressing at his chest, I wrapped my legs around his waist.

"You on birth control?" he checked. "I don't have any condoms. Really wasn't expecting you to be here."

For some reason, the way he said that suggested I was the only woman he'd consider having sex with. I knew that wasn't the case, but I also didn't want to think about another woman experiencing what he'd just done to me. Getting out of my head, I confirmed that I was on birth control.

His lips returned to mine, and the fact that he was being so patient turned me on even more. He didn't make me feel like I was a conquest he wanted to explore or a bucket for his cum. By the time he finally undressed and pressed his head to my opening, I was literally trembling in anticipation. There wasn't a part of my body he hadn't kissed, licked, or touched. The nibbles to my nipples and neck were my undoing, and I found myself begging him to come inside.

Inch by inch, Merc slowly stretched my pussy to fit his long, thick dick. That curve was *phenomenal.* It had my lips trembling from the first stroke.

I don't know... a part of me thought he'd be fast and rough. But the way Merc took his time in my pussy made me fall in love with his dick. The eye contact, the kisses, the slow... long... strokes. I could barely breathe.

With a chuckle, Merc lowered himself to my lips and asked me, "You not gon' breathe, baby?"

Quiet grunts and whimpers released from me as I lifted my arms and squeezed the pillow. I couldn't breathe. It was too overwhelming. Not just the physical, but the mental and emotional connection too. I'd never had such a present lover. Merc kept me in my body, head, and heart... and I felt everything on a deeper level.

"You gon' die 'bout this dick?" he teased, circling his hips.

When he pulled out, I muttered, "If I die, I die."

His laughter didn't stop his rhythm. My laughter did make him moan. Merc licked his lips before kissing mine.

"Breathe, baby. Don't hold your breath and fight it. I want you to feel every inch of me."

"I do." I whimpered, but I pulled in a deep breath. The moment I did, my back arched, and body warmed. "Ahh... Mercury."

"Mhm." He moaned against my neck before biting it. "Stop fighting it. You can cum. I ain't stopping no time soon."

And so I did.

And me cumming didn't pull out his.

Merc stayed in my pussy and made me cum twice more before he came.

By the time he pulled himself out of me, I was somehow depleted of my energy yet full. Maybe because I was now full of his. Either way, I was scared as fuck. Now that we'd crossed that line, how the *hell* was I supposed to stay away from this man?

I could tell Marz was tired before even asking him. He was seated at the breakfast table with his forehead in the palm of his hand. It seemed the country way of life was starting to get to him. On this trip, they had him doing more work and not just playing, and it was clear my son was not about that farm life. As amused as I was, I kept a straight face as I asked him, "You aight, little man? It looks like you're about to fall asleep."

With a slow bob of his head, Marz sat upright. "I'm all right, Daddy. Just a little tired."

Unable to hold my chuckle back, I laughed as I told him, "Eat your cereal then take a nap. If anyone tries to make you do anything else today, tell them your daddy said no. And if they got a problem with that, they can call me."

"Yes, sir." He agreed with a smile before starting on his cereal.

Aries picked up the phone, and as soon as I saw her face and heard her say, "Hey," I ended the call. I wasn't ready to be cordial with her yet. Anything I said right now was bound to hurt her feelings, so it was best if I remained silent. Neo refilled my coffee mug then sat on my lap.

"Why you hang up in her face, Mercury?"

"'Cause I ain't got shit nice to say to her."

"You aren't nice; you're genuine and kind, remember?" Sucking my teeth, I tilted my head and released a hard breath. "Be kind, baby. Maybe she was going to say something you wanted or needed to hear." Neo placed a kiss on my lips. "Call her back."

I didn't have to because she called me. For a while, I just stared at the phone.

"Mercury."

"Aight, aight."

I answered the call and put it on speaker. "What, Aries?"

"Did the call disconnect?"

"Yeah, because I disconnected it."

She scoffed. "I don't understand why you're so upset with me. You act like I'm taking Marz to a different country. Atlanta is a short drive away."

"That's not the point. You made a decision concerning our son with another nigga. You would have to transfer him to another school and get him adjusted to a life without me and our families. I'm not about to be no weekend daddy. Marz is used to having both of us every day, and you're about to destroy that. All for a nigga who wants to rap? How old is he? Twelve?"

Neo massaged her temple and shook her head with a smile, but I was dead serious. She rubbed my back, and though the gesture did calm me, it wasn't enough for me to soften my stance.

"That's not fair, Merc. If you were my husband and we

needed to leave town so you could pursue your dream, I'd go with you."

"Yeah, but he ain't your husband. And keeping it a buck, your husband would need to already be living his dream before he even married you. What kind of nigga would ask his pregnant fiancée to leave home with her five-year-old son? The fuck kind of sense does that make?"

She sighed into the receiver. "I'm not trying to argue with you. I was just calling to see if you wanted to still take Marz to Orlando later in the week. Omar wants to go and look at apartments in Atlanta."

"I can't. I'm snowed in at the cabin. If you need to, you can take him to my parents, and I'll get him when I can."

"Okay, I'll let you know."

After disconnecting the call, I laughed. "I feel like I'm in a nightmare. There's no way this girl is serious about this shit."

"She seems to really be in love."

"*Too* in love. It's like she's blind to everything else."

"That's how it be sometimes. You can be so caught up in the good that you can't see the bad." That was true. "Try not to get too anxious about it. From the sound of things, they don't have any solid plans in place yet, so there's still time for this situation to turn around."

"Maybe, but I'm not going to wait for it to turn around. I'm going to turn it around myself."

I patted her thigh so she could get up, then I grabbed my blunt and stepped outside to smoke. It was cold as hell, but I needed the relief. When I was done, I felt a slight sense of peace. I found Neo in the bathroom, getting ready to do her hair. To take my mind off things, I offered to help. I sprayed and conditioned her scalp before she pulled her locs up in a bun that gave me an unobstructed view of her beautiful face.

Time flew by as we talked and listened to music. By the time we were done, my heart was more at ease. I was glad she was here with me because she made everything feel like something I could handle, and God knows I was grateful for that.

Day 3

"It's done," Bully said. "Both."

"Aight, let 'em know I appreciate 'em."

"Always."

I disconnected the call, grateful my homies were just as loyal as I was.

I didn't plan to tell Neo what I planned to have done to Steven and his baby mama. Come to find out, ol' girl had a clothing store. It was easy to send my people out on a get back mission for her. They destroyed her inventory just like she'd done Neo's with Steven. For him, I couldn't resist letting Toe get at his ass. I told him to do lightwork so Neo wouldn't feel bad about it if Steven called her—mostly body shots that would leave him sore and bruised for a couple of weeks.

Neo hadn't been eating. I thought it was because she was depressed. When I went searching for her to give her an update on the weather, I heard a muffled version of her voice coming from one of the guest rooms. I went inside, and when I realized she was in the closet, I was about to leave. Hearing her say my name caused me to stop.

She was praying... for me.

Pressing my ear against the door, I listened as she ended her prayer with, "God, I'm ending my fast today, trusting You to be You. You are a covenant keeper. You won't go against Your nature and Your word to make a liar out of me. I'm asking that You be Jehovah Baal Perazim for Mercury. Be his Lord of breakthrough. Give him clarity, liberty, and opportunity when this snow melts. Give him clarity on how to handle this situation with Aries. Give him liberty from the thoughts and depression that have been consuming him at the mere thought of his son moving away. Give him the opportunity to restore the healthy relationship he had with Aries and bless it to be free of ego and pride and selfishness so they can be on the same page to do what's best for their son. In Jesus name I pray, amen."

Quickly shuffling out of the room, I weakly fell against the wall outside. Neo wasn't just praying for me; she'd been fasting for me too. And she wasn't doing it for show. She wasn't doing it to make herself look better in my eyes. She hadn't even mentioned it to me.

I wiped a quickly fallen tear and released a shaky breath as I stepped into the nearest guest bathroom to compose myself. Outside of my mother and grandmother, no woman had ever prayed for me. No woman had ever sacrificed and offered more of herself to God for me. No woman had ever gone to God on my behalf.

A while ago, I said there was no woman in my life worth the effort and sacrifice of being a priority. Neo had officially changed that. She wasn't just a woman I now knew my heart and body would be safe with; she was a woman I knew my soul and spirit would be safe with too.

A Few Hours Later

I WAS STARVING and couldn't wait to finish dinner. Fasting for Merc wasn't in my plans, but I felt led to do it. Merc had been nothing but good to me since the night we met, and seeing him in so much pain because of Aries and his son cracked my heart. So I'd been fasting, and it was finally over. I wanted to break my fast with something light, but I'd been craving bread for the past two days. As I lightly seasoned the marinara sauce that was simmering on the stove, I felt Merc's eyes on me. He'd been staring at me all googly eyed today, and I wasn't sure why.

Turning to face him, I chuckled. "You're being weird."

"Me?" he confirmed, making me laugh again.

"Yeah, you. Why are you staring at me? Do I have something on my face?"

"Just beauty."

With a bashful roll of my eyes, I turned and stirred the

sauce. I was going to top it with loads of parmesan and mozzarella cheese and eat it with homemade garlic toast before getting started on dinner. Merc always cooked for me and others, so I wanted to cook for him. I wasn't sure what I was going to cook yet, but he had chicken thighs, ground beef, and shrimp thawed, so it would be something with one of those.

"Don't flirt with me," I requested softly.

"Why not?"

"Because we're just friends."

He stood and made his way behind me as I removed the toast from the oven.

"Were we just friends when you were cumming on my dick and asking for more?"

Just the thought had my pussy leaking. It had been hell abstaining from food and him, but I was sure it was worth it. Besides, I didn't want us being confined here to blur the line of friendship drawn between us more than it already was.

"That was a onetime slip; it won't happen again."

"What if I want it to?" He turned me to face him. "Again and again."

Between the heat from the stove and the heat from his body, my breathing grew ragged.

"I'm not sure what's going on with you, but we agreed to be friends."

"Things change."

When I tried to walk around him, his arms gripped the oven handle and locked me in place. Closing my eyes, I pulled in a deep breath.

"You're right, things do change. And now, I never want to be with a man who has children who aren't mine again. So... cut whatever is on... off."

Merc chuckled and licked those sexy, juicy lips. Lord knew I was trying my hardest to maintain control, but the longer he stared at me with those tight, dark eyes, the more willing I was to submit to whatever it was he wanted.

"I ain't nothing like that nigga. I ain't been a cheater, and I for damn sure won't start with you." Finally, he dropped his arms and put some space between us. "You were patient with me, though, so I'll be patient with you."

I would accept that for now because I was sure when we were able to go our separate ways that whatever he was feeling would wear off. I stacked the toast up and put it on a plate then put the sauce in a round foil pan and topped it with the cheese. After a few minutes in the oven on broil, it was perfect. Once I had everything set up on the island, I poured us both a glass of wine. He said grace for what we would eat now and later, then we dug in.

"If you could be anywhere right now, where would it be?" I asked between bites.

"Orlando with my son. What about you?"

"Heaven Can Wait." His brows wrinkled, causing me to laugh softly and elaborate. "It's a vacation property in Knysna, South Africa."

"Oh, okay. Have you been there before?"

"No. I went to Africa on a mission trip when I was a teenager, but it was with family and a few members of my church. It's been popping up on my TikTok and looking like the perfect escape from everything back home. Have you been to Africa before?"

"Yeah, I've been to Zimbabwe. I want to take Marz eventually, but this Heaven Can Wait place sounds cool too."

I grabbed my phone and showed it to him, and he was

just as amazed as I was. "Can you imagine going to sleep and waking up to a view like this?"

"Damn. I'd never want to leave."

"I know, right?" I agreed with a giggle.

We continued to talk about the places we'd traveled to and experiences we had, which led to us talking about future plans, goals, and motivations. I admired the fact that he wanted to distance himself from not just illegal organizations but dangerous security jobs too. Even if it was for Marz's sake, everyone in Merc's life would benefit from it, because they'd have the peace of mind that came from knowing his every day job wasn't putting his life on the line.

"So what do you plan to do now?" I asked as we wrapped up our little snack.

"I want to open a training academy. I have a group call scheduled with a few of my guys tomorrow, actually. If I can get them to agree to teach a few classes, I'll be able to bring in more students at a time. Even though I can do it all on my own, community is big to me, so I'd like for them to be a part of it too."

"That's really cool. I'm sure it's going to be great. And Marz will be happy to have more of your time I bet."

Merc chuckled with a bob of his head. "If he'll be in Memphis, yeah. He understood I had to work, and we had a good schedule in place, but not all of my jobs were as easy as Rey's. With some clients, I had to be with them twenty-four-seven and would miss days or months away from my little man. So I'm excited to finally be done with that and moving into something more stable. He's getting older now, and I want him to see me as not just a provider but as a present father too."

It was crazy how different the person made your

perception of a situation. With Steven, him being a father was an inconvenience most of the time. My intuition was telling me something was off, but I didn't think it was him cheating with Asia. With Merc, I loved and admired the love he had for his son and enjoyed hearing him express his devotion.

"What do you plan to spend your time doing when we get back to Memphis? How'd you end up in Massie Manor anyway?"

With a chuckle, I stood to wrap up the bread and sauce. "I genuinely don't know, Merc. I was driving and so deep in my thoughts I just... didn't stop. The snow getting so bad is the only reason I stopped when I did. I guess I was going to drive until I needed gas then head home. And as far as what I'm going to do when I get back... I'm not sure. If I reopen the store, I'll need to find a new business and get new inventory, which means I'll have to get a loan. I have money saved now, but my parents stressed to me the importance of not living above my means. As quickly as I want to reopen, I won't do it by draining my savings account. I have to move with order. So, I'll stay with them until I find my own place, and once I have that secured, then I'll focus on the store."

"Have you considered drop shipping until you can get another storefront?"

"I have... but I love the experience of my store, you know? I wasn't just selling vinyl records. I loved talking to my people, listening to music, and allowing my space to be used for open mic nights and concerts. I'm just like you are about community, and music is what tied me to mine. So I could operate online, but it just wouldn't be the same."

"Well..." Merc licked the corner of his mouth as he stood. "I pray God gives you clarity and understanding on what it is you need to do when we get home." He closed the space between us, and when my head lowered to hide my blush, he lifted it and cupped my cheek. "I pray He keeps in the forefront of your mind that you have the liberty to reinvent your life right now, and there's no need to rush into one particular thing. And I pray He gives you opportunities to not only reopen your store but reconnect with your community and highlight local artists so you all can do what you love... what you were purposed to do."

My mouth opened and closed, but all I could do was chuckle because those were the exact words I'd used in my prayer for him earlier. Either we were more in sync than I'd realized, or he heard me... and that was why he'd been acting all weird today.

"Amen," I said. "You heard me earlier?"

With a smile, Merc tilted my head and gave me a sweet, quick kiss. "I did."

"Why didn't you say anything?"

"Even though it was about me and my situation, I felt like that was a moment between you and God. But I meant every word I just said, and I'm truly grateful for you not only praying for me but fasting for me as well. Knowing that I can trust you spiritually when it comes to myself and my son means more to me than you will ever know. And that's exactly why I don't care about you not wanting to be with a man that has kids, because you're mine."

"Mercury... I..."

Groaning, I watched him leave the kitchen. He had a way of making it clear he was done with a situation or conversation that couldn't be denied. I wouldn't stop him from trying to pursue me, but I really didn't see my mind changing. What happened with Steven was too fresh. As much as I liked Merc, I didn't see him being able to do anything to change that.

AFTER DINNER, we watched a movie together before showering and getting in bed. This was the most relaxed I'd been in a long time, and Merc said the same for himself. Even with the weight of everything that awaited us when we got back home, I was grateful for this brief intermission that came because of the snowstorm.

Everything in Massie Manor was shut down. The roads kept icing over because the temperature was so low at night. It was projected that we'd have another two or three days here before the ice started to melt enough for us to leave, and I was okay with that.

"What you wanna watch now?" Merc asked.

As much as I wanted to say his dick sliding in and out of my pussy, I held those words back. I'd been craving him since I ended my fast, and I wasn't sure why. I felt like it was the desire of my flesh amplified because I was finally able to indulge if I wanted to, but I was trying not to. Having sex with him would only make me like and want him more.

Before I could answer, my phone vibrated on the night-stand. The sight of my mom's picture made me smile. I accepted her FaceTime request and greeted her with, "Hey, Ma."

"Hey, baby. I was just checking on you."

"I'm good. What y'all doing?"

"Getting ready to eat some soup I made yesterday. It's not snowing here, but we had a cold front from the snow y'all got in Massie Manor. How's Merc?"

"He's fine."

"Tell 'im I said he better be taking care of my baby," Daddy said in the background.

"I always will," Merc replied.

"Well, I'll let you go," Ma said with a cheesy grin. "But we need to talk when you get back home."

Chuckling, I slipped further into the bed. "About what?"

"How you keep getting caught up with that man you're in bed with. Y'all sleeping together... or *sleeping* together?"

"Maaa," I dragged, causing them all to laugh. "Goodbye."

"Bye, baby," she said through her laugh. "And bye, Merc."

"Bye, Mrs. Tina."

I disconnected the call quickly. "Ugh. She's so embarrassing."

"You asked," Merc said with a snicker.

"Yeah, and I shouldn't have. She probably would have said more if I let her."

Merc took my hand into his and kissed it. "I don't think it's a coincidence that you came here to me. You might not want to accept it because your heart is hurting right now, but you were led to me for a reason."

Swallowing hard, I looked over at him with watery eyes. "I'm not sure what that reason could be."

"I am." Merc hovered over me and pulled me closer. "It's so I can heal that pain with my love."

When he lowered his lips to mine, I happily accepted the kiss. Suddenly, watching another movie was the last thing on my mind. We spent the rest of the night kissing, cuddling, and talking... and by the time we went to sleep... my heart was full.

"I'm ready for whatever," Asylum said. "The way you've shown up for me with my asylums, you know you can get whatever out of me, brotha."

"Same," Bully said.

"Just let us know what you need us to do," Karrington added.

"Fa sho," Beethoven replied.

"That's love. I appreciate y'all, for real," I said. "I'ma get a draft together while I'm here and hit the ground running when I get back to Memphis. After I get everything finalized with my business coach, I'll let y'all know."

"Aye," Karrington called before I could end the call. "You still uh... use Luna Ray for your business coach?"

We all chuckled. The fact that Karrington called LuLu by her government name was proof that he liked her, but unfortunately, he didn't step up when he needed to, and she married and had a son with someone else. Since then, Karrington hadn't been in a serious relationship. I felt like it was because he was waiting for LuLu. I couldn't imagine how it felt trying to replace the best woman you'd ever had and watching her be with someone else.

"Yeah, I do. She hasn't been working a lot since she had her son, but she still has sessions with previous clients."

"Oh. Okay. Well... when you talk to her, tell her I hope she's well."

"This nigga," Toe grumbled.

"Don't start with that shit," Karrington said, and we all laughed.

"Mane, if you'on go get ya girl," Bully demanded.

"How, nigga?" Asylum asked. "She's married."

"So? That's just a piece of paper. Her Kare Bear has her heart."

"On that note, I'm out," Karrington said with a smile and shake of his head before disconnecting on his end.

"You was wrong for that," I told Bully through my laugh.

"It was the truth though," Toe agreed.

We talked a few minutes more before I thanked them again and ended the call.

I took a few moments to write some notes down before going to find my girl. She was in the guest room where all the games were, playing Mahjong. I told her to come find me when she was done so we could go out and play in the snow, and her entire face brightened like I knew it would. She was down to do it now, so I gave her some of my clothes to put on since she was ill prepared for such cold weather. My sweats and hoodie drowned her, but like always, she was cute.

"You need these," she said as I put my beanie over her head and slid my gloves onto her tiny hands.

"I'll be good. I just want to make sure you don't get sick."

I wasn't expecting it, but I gladly welcomed it when she gripped my chin and lowered me to her for a kiss. Wrapping my arms around her waist, I pulled her closer and slipped my tongue into her mouth. The sweet sighs she released were like music to my ears. This girl was making a lover out of me.

"What was that for so I can make sure I do it again?" I asked, making her laugh.

"For being kind and a gentleman." Neo gave me another kiss. "Caring and considerate." And another one. "For just being you." And another one.

"You gon' run away from me when this is over?"

Her head shook softly as her hands slid down my chest. "I don't intend to. But if I do... just pull me back."

That was cool with me, because I had no problem chasing her and earning her... making sure she knew she was safe with me in all ways, not just physically.

We made our way outside, and it felt good as hell to feel the sun on my face, even though it was so cold. Building snowmen turned into a snowball fight, which led to us falling over onto each other and not being in a rush to get up. When we finally did, we went back inside, and I got us a pot of coffee going.

Once we were warmed up, we spent a little time apart which had become our routine, and it was one I appreciated. When we did come back into each other's orb, it was to make chili on Facebook live. Innvy had tuned in, and she was with Bully, so we spent the bulk of the time talking to them. After we had dinner, the TV watched us as we talked about our flaws and fears.

"I wouldn't think a man like you had fears," she admitted, sipping her hot tea with a shot of whiskey.

"Fear is an emotion. We all have those."

"That's true." A beat of silence passed before she asked, "What do you need from your life partner?"

"The fact that you said life partner instead of girlfriend is the biggest thing. A true partner, which in itself is a list of things." She nodded her agreement. "Excitement, support, friendship, acceptance, appreciation, respect, trust, love."

Neo chuckled. "Why is love last?"

"That's what means the least to me," I admitted. "I know it's the opposite for you as a woman, but it means more to me that you respect and trust me than love me. I want to be loved, and I'll honor it, but without that other stuff, it means nothing."

"You're right about that. I was so focused on Steven's love that I didn't pay attention to the fact that so many other things were missing from our relationship and him as a man. He didn't respect me or the commitment we made. Being faithful wasn't his desire nor was it in his character. That's why there's no part of me that feels like there was anything I did wrong to warrant that. It hurts, I ain't gon' lie, but I know that was a reflection of him... not me."

"Hell yeah." I agreed. "When a man is truly locked in, a woman shouldn't even have the chance to get close enough to think she has an opening. It's disrespectful to even flirt, to me, while you're in a relationship. My woman gon' always feel secure with me, and I ain't lettin' a woman on the outside make my woman question her place in my life. That's why if you ever cheated on me, it better be with a nigga you don't value 'cause his fade gettin' slid back when I see 'im."

"Whoa, wait." Her hands lifted as she laughed like I was playing, but I was serious as a motherfucker. "That took a very violent and aggressive turn."

"I'm a violent and aggressive nigga."

Her constant giggle made me smile, no matter how much I needed her to understand I was serious. If she cheated on me, I'd handle her how I saw fit, but it was off with that nigga's *head*. I'd hold her accountable because she let a man have access to what should have been reserved for me and me alone, but no man would be able to walk this earth and be able to say he had what belonged to me.

"I'm not your woman, so I don't know why you made that personal and said if *I* cheat. I'm not a cheater, though, despite what our first kiss suggested."

"I know you're not. If it wasn't me, it wouldn't have happened. The fact that you went against your character to have me should prove to you even more what's up between us. And you *are* my woman."

"When did we establish this title?" she asked with a sexy, syrupy smile.

"Titles honor men, but they don't really matter to me because I don't need the validation. We locked in because you've honored and respected me without one. So you're mine."

Our eyes remained locked as she straddled me.

"Say it again," she demanded, sliding her hand into my sweats.

"You're mine."

"And you're mine?" Between her hand stroking my dick, her sexy voice, and hypnotic stare... all I could do was nod as I bit down on my lip. "Say it. Tell me you're mine."

"I'm yours, Neo."

With a moan, she placed my hands on her body, and that was all the invitation I needed to become one with her again. In the past, pussy was pussy. All it was to me, was a release. It didn't rule me like most men who lacked discipline and control. There were other pleasures that I valued more. But Neo's pussy? Neo's pussy held power.

As she slid down on my dick, I had to keep her from moving so I wouldn't cum immediately. It felt like I was back home after a long voyage, and I couldn't rush this release.

"I missed you," she muttered against my lips before kissing me.

"You never have to. This dick is yours too."

"Only mine?"

"Mhm." She had no fucking idea. I didn't want anyone before her, and there was no doubt in my mind that I'd want anyone after her. My dick wouldn't either.

"You promise?"

"I promise, baby. All of me is yours."

That seemed to satisfy her, because she wrapped her arms around me and began a slow and steady ride. Outside of reminding her to breathe, no words were spoken between us. We let our connection do the talking. Her pussy molded against my dick like it was made for me. Like *she* was made for me. And there was no doubt in my mind that our time together at this cabin was meant to solidify that.

Two Days Later

SAINT HAD WARMED MY HEART. He was becoming the big brother I'd never had. Music had bound us, but our connection was growing deeper than that. I was on the phone with Harmony, and we were updating each other on our lives. When he heard about what Steven and Asia had done to my store, I had to beg him not to go pull up on him.

My dad and cousins wanted to do the same thing, but I didn't want them getting into trouble because of me. Merc didn't tell me what his people had done, but it must have been something because Steven blew my phone up so much, I had to block him. Before we'd even gotten off the phone, Saint had sent ten thousand dollars to my Venmo in two transactions for me to rebuild my inventory. He also offered any room I wanted in his nonprofit building, In Harmony, for me to use for any events I wanted to have until I reopened my store.

I cried like a baby before getting off the phone. Saint had always been that kind of man. He didn't talk much; he was a man of action. I didn't ask anything of him, but God blessed me through him out of the kindness of his heart.

Once I washed my face and composed myself, I went to find Merc. He was on a FaceTime call with Marz. I was going to leave them alone, but Merc called me over to see Marz.

"Hi, cutie," I spoke with a wave. He looked so cute in his little cowboy hat.

"Hi, ma'am."

"Aww, aren't you a little gentleman, just like your daddy." Marz's eyes shifted toward Merc, who was grinning with pride. "I hear you like animals."

"I do!" Marz sat up in his seat. "I think horses are my favorite. Do you like animals?"

"I love animals. I'm scared of horses though."

"You are?" He giggled, covering his snaggle-toothed smile. "Why?"

"Well, when I tried to learn how to ride one, it bucked a little too hard and I fell off."

Marz gasped before laughing again. "Did it hurt?"

"A lot." I laughed. "I haven't tried again since that."

"What we say about fear?" Merc asked.

"It's just an emotion, and our emotions can lead us, but we have to navigate them logically."

"Exactly. Aye, Marz," Merc said, redirecting his attention to his son, "you wanna teach Ms. Neo how to ride a horse?"

"Ooh, that'll be fun! Yes! I know all about horses now."

I chuckled as Merc said, "Aight, so when it gets a little cooler in Jasper Lane, I'll take you to Karrington's ranch, and you can show her what you got."

"Awesome!" he yelled, pumping his fist. "Don't worry, Ms. Neo. I won't let you fall."

His declaration warmed my heart. He was gonna be a little protector, just like his dad. A few kids yelled for Marz, and he darted out of the room. Aries grabbed the phone, and that was my cue to give them some privacy. I tried to leave, but Merc pulled me onto his lap.

"Oh, hey," Aries said through her chuckle. It was obvious she was surprised by the gesture, but I didn't get a sense of anything negative.

"Hi."

"Aries, this is Neo. Neo, this is Aries."

"It's nice to virtually meet you," she said with a warm smile.

"Same. You have a handsome son, and he's sweet and gentle yet protective, just like his dad."

"I know. I was truly blessed." Her hand lowered to her belly as she said, "I'm hoping this one will come out just as good."

"You're having another boy?" I asked.

"I don't know yet." She released a tired sigh. "Just hoping for the best either way."

"I feel you. As long as they are healthy, that's all that truly matters."

Aries nodded her agreement. "Well... I just wanted to call so Marz could see his dad. I won't hold y'all. Y'all be safe out there."

"You taking him to my parents?" Merc asked, rubbing my thigh.

"Nah. I convinced Omar to wait until next week to go look at apartments."

"Good. I'm glad to see you're finally using your influence for good."

With a playful grin and roll of her eyes, Aries looked away. "Bye, Merc."

"Bye."

He disconnected the call and kissed my shoulder. "What can I do to make sure you trust there's nothing going on sexually or romantically between me and Aries?"

"Honestly, I don't know. Assurance is one thing, but if your actions when we're apart don't align, it means nothing." I was sure that wasn't the answer he was expecting, but it was all I had to give. I didn't know what he could say to make me trust them or what he could do. "Maybe if I knew y'all history, that would help."

"Well, we dated for a year and decided we were better off as friends. We didn't have any of the same interests and hobbies. And in the case of opposites attract, there wasn't much binding us and keeping us together. With the recreational intimacy missing, we weren't spending a lot of time together, so that caused a lot of static." He paused and chuckled. "Ironically, when we agreed to break up, that's when we found out she was pregnant. We got back together and tried again, but just after Marz turned one, we broke up for good. So in four years, we haven't been in a relationship or had sex. She's been with other men, obviously, and I've dated other women and had sex, but I haven't committed to anyone."

"Why not? Because they can't top her?"

"Not at all. I haven't been committed because no woman has been worth it. I've dedicated myself to my son and work. Now I won't lie and say I haven't prioritized Aries, because I have. She's an extension of my son, so I've taken care of her over the years, but it's been out of love and respect for her being the mother of my little man, nothing more."

"How do you... take care of her? What does her place in your life look like?"

He didn't answer right away, and I was glad he was careful with his words and tone for this conversation. His expressions and energy didn't give annoyed with my questioning, and that made me feel like I'd be safe to express my concerns with him.

"They live in the mother-in-law suite behind my house, so she's stable because of me. Aries doesn't work. I wanted her to be able to take care of our son and have the time to still enjoy her life, whether she wanted to do that with rest, play, or starting her own business. I pay her bills to ensure she's good because, in turn, my son is good too. We had a very healthy coparenting relationship until she started dating Omar, then it started to get a little... off. It didn't get bad until he proposed though."

"Okay, thank you for sharing."

"I know there might not be one thing I can say or do to get you to trust that all of you is safe with me, but if you give us a chance, I promise you won't regret it. My time with Aries has passed. The only thing tying us together is our son. I have no romantic feelings for her. The only woman I want to be with romantically is sitting on my lap."

Resting my forehead on his, I admitted, "This helped a little."

Merc chuckled as he wrapped his arms around me. "Good. I don't care if you have to hear me say that a million times, I will. I don't want anyone else but you, baby. And I'm going to show you that every day that I have you."

I covered his lips with mine, but the sound of a large truck caused me to pull away. We went to the living room window and watched as a snowplow slowly pushed snow forward.

"Well, it looks like we'll be out of here soon," he said.

"I was so ready to leave when I first got here."

"And now?"

"I want another day."

Pulling me close, he kissed my forehead then my lips. "Then we'll take another day."

Early March

Since Neo's car had been under the snow for so long, I had it towed to her parents' place to be safe, and she came to my home. I gave her a tour since I was unable to the first time. I was proud of the life I'd built for me and my son and hoped Neo would be a part of that. I wasn't naïve enough to believe it would be easy for her to trust me with what had just happened with her ex, but I hoped she was wise enough to see the differences between us and know I was nothing like him.

As we got settled into my home theater, my phone rang. It was Aries. I answered with, "Y'all good?"

"Yes. Are you home yet? We're in Memphis. I was going to bring Marz to you."

"Yeah, I'm back. Bring my little man home."

"Okay, we'll be there in like thirty minutes."

"Aight, cool."

I hadn't even disconnected the call all the way before Neo was saying, "I'm gonna take an Uber to my parents' house so you can spend some time with Marz."

"Neo..."

"I mean it, Mercury. We've spent the last week together, and though I enjoyed every second of it, I know you missed your son like crazy."

I couldn't argue with her because that was the truth. "If you're sure, I can drop you off real quick."

"You sure, babe?"

"I'm positive."

"Okay, that'll work."

As much as I was enjoying our time together, I was grateful she wasn't the kind of woman who expected me to choose between her and my son. They would always lose. Had she stayed, I would have made sure she was entertained while I gave my attention to Marz, but now, I wouldn't have to.

Marz wasn't trying to go to sleep. He was clearly tired and could barely hold his eyes open after I finished his bedtime story. It wasn't like him to fight his sleep, especially if he was excited about something the next day. We were going to my parents' house, and they spoiled him and never told him no.

"You okay, little man?" I asked, rubbing his head. He nodded then shook his head. I returned to my seat on the side of his bed. "What's wrong, son?"

He looked away briefly. "Mommy said we were moving away with Mr. Omar, but I don't want to. I don't want to leave you and my grandma and paw paw. Or Kiana and my friends at school."

I had to work really hard to keep my face from showing how I was feeling, because I didn't want him to think my anger was over what he'd said. I couldn't believe Aries told Marz they were moving before we'd made a final decision. And even if we had made a decision, that was a conversation we needed to have with him together. Yet again, she was moving as if Omar was her husband and the father of her child and leaving me out of it, and that shit was disrespectful as fuck and pissing me off. Clearly, since telling her that wasn't getting through her thick ass skull, I would have to tell her man and make sure he never had a conversation about my son's future without me being present again.

"You're not going anywhere, Marz. Don't even worry about that, aight?"

"But Mommy said..."

"That don't matter. I'm telling you that you aren't leaving. Okay?"

With a nod, he pulled his covers up to his chin. "Yes, sir."

"Get some sleep, and don't worry about that. Daddy's gonna handle it."

Marz smiled as I gave him a kiss on the cheek.

"I love you, Daddy."

"I love you more. Good night."

"Night."

I would usually wait until he was asleep to leave his room, but I couldn't wait to get out of there fast enough tonight. I went outside to the mother-in-law suite, where Aries and Omar were chilling in the living room, watching a movie.

"Merc, wh—ah!"

Aries yelled as I popped Omar in his mouth. The groan he released was silenced by another hit. It wasn't hard enough to knock him out because I needed him to hear me well. My fist wrapped around his shirt, and I used it to lift him off the couch.

"Your fiancée don't seem to understand the rules around this bitch when it comes to my son. Y'all don't make decisions without me, and y'all don't have important conversations if I'm not present without my approval. If I hear that you've done it again, I'ma beat yo' ass, and if you do it a third time, I'ma slit yo' throat and you won't be able to talk no mo'. Do you fuckin' hear me?"

"Yeah, man," he rushed out quickly.

Tossing him back onto the couch, I gave Aries my attention. "Why you tell my son he was moving?"

"I—"

"You tryin' my fuckin' patience, Aries." I interrupted before she could even answer. "I been giving you grace out of respect, but that shit is dead. Since you can't give the same back, it's ova. You know how I come, so since you want to get a judge involved, we can do that, 'cause I'm real close to sending yo' second baby daddy to God just to teach you not to play with me."

"But, Merc, I..."

I pointed my finger toward her as I took deep breaths. "Stop fucking playing with me, Aries. For real."

Snapping her mouth shut, she nodded adamantly. My eyes went back to Omar as he used his shirt to wipe the blood that was leaking from his mouth.

"Your ass can't come over here no more. You getting too comfortable. Take her to your house when y'all want to kick it or put some' on the fucking rent. Get the fuck out. Both of y'all."

Neither of them hesitated to grab their shit and scramble out the room. Plopping down on the couch, I took deep breaths and rocked until I was calm. I chuckled in disbelief that this had become my life. I wanted Aries to move on and find love but not at the expense of our ability to coparent in a healthy way for the sake of our son. Of all the men she could have chosen, I wasn't sure what the hell Omar had said and done to hook her. The shit was truly beyond me.

When I went back into the house, I took out my stash and lit up a blunt, resisting the urge to tell Neo to come to me. I didn't want to pile my drama on to her, so I'd spend the evening alone, but Lord knew I needed her peace to consume me.

ne Week Later

I WAS HAVING such a good time with Merc's parents, Porsha and Frank, that it was scary. Marz was truly a small replica of his father. They all had welcomed me in with open arms, making my first visit to his parents' home a success. We'd spent the evening having dinner and talking. When it was over, the music started up, and like a true southern family, it led to drinking and dancing.

He'd told his mom I was into embroidery, and she knitted, so we'd made a date to do both tomorrow. As good of a time as I was having, I couldn't stop myself from blurting, "I don't want to fall in love with you." My eyes watered, causing me to avoid his.

Merc probably thought I was crazy. I'd just told him how much fun I'd had as we left the house. Now, at his car, I was on the verge of having an emotional breakdown.

"I wouldn't let you," Merc admitted. I looked into his

eyes. “Falling suggests an accident. Something unintentional.” He stepped in front of me and tilted my head by my chin. “I’m going to be very intentional with everything I do to make you grow in love with me.”

Nibbling my bottom lip, I blinked back my tears.

Merc kissed me tenderly, pulling me off the car and into his embrace.

“Does that sound okay with you, baby?” he asked, and between his smooth tone and charming smile, I would have agreed, even if I didn’t want to.

“Yes,” I almost whispered before going in for another kiss.

“Thank you.”

“For what?”

“Being vocal when you were overwhelmed instead of staying in your head about it.”

I chuckled as I placed my hands on his chest. “Yeah. As we left out, I was thinking about how much fun I had and how much I could love your family. Then I started thinking about how much I could love you. And that scared the shit out of me.”

“It doesn’t have to. I’ma keep saying this like an affirmation until it sticks in your head and your heart. You’re safe with me, Neo. In all ways.”

That pulled me off the ledge, so I nodded and gave him another hug. Merc opened the door and let me inside. Our drive to his home was filled with singing and rapping along to his ’90s playlist. I knew we were going to have a good time tonight when he stopped by Beethoven’s place to reup on his personal stash of marijuana.

When we made it to his home, Aries was seated in the living room, waiting for him.

"I'll uh... give you two some space," I said, preparing to head to his room.

"Nah, you can stay," Merc said. "She don't mind putting Omar in our business, so I don't mind putting you in ours."

I felt like he was saying that to be petty. He'd told me about what happened when we first came back. I didn't want to be used as a pawn between them, but I also wouldn't leave him if he didn't want me to. We all sat down, and I felt so awkward, listening in on their conversation.

Well, if they would even have a conversation. Aries immediately broke into tears. I wanted to console her, but since I didn't really know her that well, I shoved Merc in her direction. With a huff, he stood and walked over to her. Seated next to her, he held her until she was all cried out. When her tears stopped, Merc stood and made his way back next to me.

"What was that about?" Merc asked, checking the time on his Rolex.

"Omar and I... we're over."

Merc smiled. I elbowed him, and he grunted before wiping his smile away.

"I'm sorry to hear that," he said, smile returning. "What happened?"

"After you assaulted him a week ago, he started acting funny."

"Wait, what?" I said, turning slightly to face Merc. "What did you do?"

"It's in the past," he grumbled, scratching his nose. "It wasn't nothing he didn't deserve, though."

Aries rolled her eyes and sat up in her seat. "He didn't deserve that, Merc, and that's the problem. You feel like because I'm the mother of your child that you have a say in everything I do. It's not fair because I don't do that to you."

"I don't feel like I have a say in everything you do, but I do have a say in everything that concerns my son. That's what you can't seem to understand. Regardless of who you marry, I'm still Marz's father. You can't make decisions for him without consulting me, Aries. I don't understand why you can't accept that."

Her shoulders slouched as she sighed. "You're right. I know that. I guess I was just... so caught up in my happiness and getting married that I didn't want to let you ruin that. When I got pregnant, the pressure to detach myself from you felt worse. So when Omar proposed and asked me to move with him to Atlanta, I agreed."

"Okay, so what happened? I know he didn't break up with you because I gave him a few punches."

"One of his teeth came out, and another one was chipped," she said through gritted teeth.

"Oop, gahdamn." I meant to mutter, but it came out louder than I'd meant for it to, causing Merc to laugh. "Sorry."

"*He's* the one that should be sorry. Omar said he wants nothing to do with you, so he basically said Marz has to stay here. He wanted me to come here to spend time with my son just to avoid you."

"And I know you weren't going for that shit," Merc said.

Aries smiled for the first time since their conversation started. "Hell nah. I told him if he didn't want my son, he didn't want me. I did admit that I hadn't been communicating properly and sticking to the boundaries you and I had in place, which caused you to show your ass. I told him if I stopped doing that, things would get back to how they used to be. That's when he straight up said I had to leave

Marz here, or we were done." She scoffed and crossed her legs. "Can you believe he told me to give him the ring back so he could use it to buy a plane ticket?"

Now that got a good laugh out of Merc. "What happened to all the money he said he had saved?"

"Apparently, that was a lie. When we were in Mississippi, he said I needed to get ready to start working again so I could help with bills. That's what led me to tell Marz about the move. I wasn't fully on board with it, but I was willing to do what I had to, to keep my family together."

"I can respect that," Merc said with a bob of his head. "So what does this mean for the little one?" he asked, pointing to her stomach.

"Now that, I don't know." Aries sighed and ran her fingers through her hair. "From the looks of it, he's leaving for good. I don't know if he plans to be here for the baby or not."

Her eyes watered and head hung. This time, I didn't have to tell Merc to go and comfort her, because he did it on his own.

"I'm sorry, Aries. For real. I wanted shit to get better, but I didn't want him to break your heart. I just... knew you deserved better than what he was offering and didn't want you to settle or put my son in an environment that wasn't healthy." He paused. "You don't have to worry about what he does. Whether he's present or not, I'll be here for you and the baby. You can still stay here until you find a man that's truly worthy of you and can provide you with the lifestyle that you and my son are used to getting from me."

"Thank you," she whimpered, hugging him tightly.

When he kissed her temple, the gesture made my eyes water. Merc was truly a standup guy, and I'd never be able to deny that. The longer they embraced, the more uncomfortable I felt. I knew Merc said there was nothing romantic between them, but my trauma was far too recent. The wound was still open, and thinking about something developing between them had my heart hurting already. This was exactly what I wanted to avoid.

Quietly, I stood and headed to Merc's room to request an Uber since he'd picked me up from my parents' home. I wasn't sure what would happen between us in the future, but I knew for right now, his hands were too full juggling his family, and I didn't know if that family would fit me.

As Aries and I released each other, she said, "Neo, I didn't mean to intrude... oh. She's gone."

I looked where Neo had been sitting then toward the hallway. "She probably just went to the room."

"Tell her I didn't mean to take up too much of your time. And thank you again, Merc, for everything. You're truly a great guy. I hope she knows what she has in you."

"She does," was what I said, and I hoped that was the truth.

After Aries left, I went to my bedroom, and Neo was there. She was seated on the sofa with her head buried in her phone.

"You didn't have to leave," I told her as I walked in her direction.

When she looked up but avoided my eyes, I knew something was wrong.

"I can't do this, baby," she whispered.

"Do what?" I asked, sitting next to her.

"This." She pointed between us. "I know you said

there's nothing between y'all, and I believe that, I really do. I've seen how great of a man you are for myself, and I know you can take care of her and the new baby and it not be a romantic gesture for you."

"Then what's the problem?"

Nibbling her bottom lip, she scooted to the side to face me fully. "All I'll be thinking about is what Steven did and how you being so good to her can make her fall in love with you. And I know that hasn't happened in the past, but things are different now. I've seen women fall in love with a man who was taking care of them and their children. That's a natural reaction to the provision."

"Even if her feelings for me did change, which they won't, it won't matter because I'm not in love with her. A baby she has with another nigga ain't gon' change that."

"I know that in my mind," she stressed, no longer able to hold back her tears. "But my heart doesn't care about that logic. It's just... too soon. I don't want to punish you for what Steven did. I can't bleed onto you because of a cut he caused. It won't be fair for my paranoia to affect what you have going on with your family here. So I think it'll be best if we stop this before it fully starts."

"I appreciate and respect that, but no."

Her brows wrinkled and head tilted as she slid her hand out of mine. "No?" Neo repeated.

"You a parrot now? I said no."

"I didn't ask you a yes or no question. I'm telling you we don't need to see each other anymore."

"And I'm telling you that ain't gon' happen." With a chuckle, I stood and headed to the closet to undress. "I'on know what the fuck you think this is, but it ain't that."

"Mercury..."

"You prayed and fasted for me. You opened my heart.

You made me start to love you. Ain't no cuttin' that shit off. If you need some time to heal so you can see me for me and not him, I'm cool with that, but this ain't over."

With a sigh, she leaned against the doorframe. "My Uber is here."

I walked over to her and gave her a lingering kiss. "Let me know when you get home, Neo."

"I was serious about what I said."

Sucking my teeth, I pulled her into my space and gave her another kiss. "Let me know when you get home. All that other shit you talkin' about really don't matter."

Her eyes rolled as she walked away. That was cool. She could have her little attitude, but it wasn't going to change shit. Neo was mine, and the sooner she accepted that, the better.

~

That Sunday Evening

"Please tell me Neo not being here all weekend isn't because of me," Aries said after I put Marz to sleep.

I hadn't had an actual conversation with Neo for the rest of the weekend. As much as I wanted to talk to her, see her, and hold her, I wanted to give her the space she needed to receive clarity on the situation. I did check in with her daily to make sure she was good, but that was it.

"Nah. She has a fresh relationship wound. The last nigga she was with cheated on her with his baby mama."

"Ouch." It wasn't funny, but Aries' pained expression made me laugh. "She really didn't need to see us have that conversation, Merc. I can't imagine how that made her feel."

My head shook as I sat next to her on the couch. "Nah, she needed to see it. I'm not going to hide the way we handle each other from my wife, whether it's good or bad."

"Your wife?" Aries repeated softly.

"She the one. I just... don't know how to get her to see that."

Her smile was soft as she rested her hand on my thigh. "It's not for her to see it first; that's on you. When you know she's the woman in the vision you have for your life, your pursuit, protection, and provision is what will allow her to see that."

Sucking my teeth, I side eyed her. "How you know all that yet let Omar have you out here going out bad?"

She laughed like I hoped she would. "Listen, we're not gonna talk about that, okay? All I can say is the dick had me in love, and I really felt like I'd taken so much from you." Her smile fell and tone grew serious. "You do more for me than is required. It's men out here who barely pay child support, yet you allow me to live here rent free, and you pay the rest of my bills. Omar and I had a genuine connection; it just wasn't one that should have led to marriage, but I didn't want to accept that. He seemed like my way of finally standing on my own two feet and not having to depend on you so much. I'm just glad you stood firm and didn't let me go out bad. I might have hated you for it, but I know you had me and Marz's best interests at heart."

"Always, and I always will. And you're not a burden on me, Aries. When we had our son, I made up in my mind to do whatever I had to do to make sure neither of you wanted for anything. It's literally nothing for me to provide for you financially. You're nurturing my son. That's the least I can do for you." Her eyes started to water, and I didn't want her to get emotional again, so I stood. "If you're craving independence, open a business. If it provides enough for you to pay your own bills, pay them hos. But it's not a requirement that you do. I meant it when I said I'll provide for you until your husband can."

Wiping a quickly fallen tear, Aries nodded. "Thank you, Merc," she almost whispered.

"You're welcome. But if you really want to thank me, fix me a banana pudding tomorrow since your ass ain't got shit else to do."

As she laughed, she tried to hit me with a pillow, but I was able to walk away.

"Get your greedy ass out, but I got you."

Once I was home and settled, I sent Neo a good night text like I'd done for the past two nights. Like the past two nights, she replied with, *good night Mercury. Pinch Marz's cheeks for me.*

How about you come do it yourself tomorrow?

Her dots popped up and stayed on the screen for a while, but she didn't respond. I'd take that. It was better than a no.

One Week Later

PRODUCTIVITY HELPED KEEP me from going after Merc even though I missed him so much. Protecting myself hurt, but it didn't hurt nearly as much as destroying my relationship with Merc would have because of Steven. It didn't matter how much I told myself they weren't the same, Merc was like a mirror. Or maybe, he was like a second chance. I didn't know if the second chance was for me to choose not to be with a man who had kids, to avoid being hurt, or if he was a second chance to prove I could be with a man who had kids and not get hurt. Either way, I didn't want to make a move until I was absolutely sure.

I'd started restocking my inventory and looking at apartments and buildings. My parents made it clear there was no rush for me to leave, but I hadn't lived at home since I was in high school and wanted my own space. As I browsed commercial listings, Ma came in and sat on the edge of my bed.

"I have a dilemma," she said, gaining my full attention.

"What's up?" I asked, closing the laptop.

"Your aunt is putting together a couple's cruise for this summer. She asked me if you were seeing anyone, and I didn't know what to say."

With a chuckle, I sat next to her. "Honestly, Ma, I don't know the answer to that either."

"Why not?"

"Because I want to be with Merc, but I just can't put myself in the position to be cheated on again."

"Has Merc done anything to make you believe he will cheat on you?"

"Quite the opposite. He's assured me and validated me. It's just a reflex to protect myself, you know?"

Her light laugh soothed me as she took my hand into hers. "I remember when you got food poisoning while you were in college. You got so sick I had to come and take care of you. You remember what you said?"

Laughing, I nodded. "I said I would never eat again."

"That lasted for what... all of a week?"

That was true. I loved to eat too much to give up food. "Where are you going with this, Ma?"

"You were hurt by food, and you wanted to avoid it forever, but you didn't. Every time you eat, you're trusting what has been prepared will not hurt you and make you sick again. Love is the same way." She paused, allowing me to fully take in what she'd said. "You can't let one bad experience with love keep you from it forever. Just because he hurt you, that doesn't mean every man you date who has children will. Let Merc be the chicken noodle soup you need for your soul. Let him be your first healthy meal after your heart was poisoned by someone else. Let his love satiate you. Get ready to feast again."

Sniffling, I pushed back my tears as she kissed my temple and gave me a hug. She stood, leaving me alone with her words. When my tears began to pour, I leaned back on the bed and stared at the ceiling.

"God, please give me a sign. I want to trust Merc and be loved by him, but I'm so scared. I don't want to move too fast and be hurt because I ignored the signs. I need to know You approve of this and that I'll be safe because we have your blessing. I need a wink, God. Show me I'm as safe with Merc as he says I am."

The doorbell rang, and since I wasn't expecting anyone, I didn't bother to get up as I wiped my face. The sound of my mother's laughter made me curious, but I still stayed in bed… until she called my name.

I made my way downstairs, and at the sight of my absolute favorite neo soul singer out of Memphis, Audré, my mouth hung open.

"Are you Neo?" she asked, smiling sweetly.

There was a man standing next to her with a large bear, balloons, and roses. I nodded because I was truly speechless.

"Ooh, let me record this!" Mama yelled, making me laugh.

"This is for you, from Merc," Audré said before she began to sing "Safe with Me" by Sam Smith. By the time she was done, tears were pouring from my eyes. She gave me a hug, then the man gave me the bear, balloons, and roses. After setting everything down, I took the note from the bouquet and read it.

I understand you need time to heal. As much as I miss you, I'll give you that, because I want nothing to stand in the way of our love. I'll wait for you, but if you're willing to take a chance, I'll love the pain out of you.

Pressing the note to my chest, I released a light chuckle. Was this my God wink?

When the doorbell rang, I wasn't expecting it to be Neo. Just like at the cabin, at the sight of me, she burst into tears. I suspected these were happy tears. It took a favor for me to get Audré to sing for her, but it was worth it. I was willing to wait for Neo, like I said, but I also wanted her to know there didn't have to be a wait.

After wrapping her legs around me, I closed and locked the door then carried her to my bedroom.

I put her on her feet in front of the bed and wiped her eyes.

"Hi," she spoke softly with a giggle.

"You good?"

"Yes. Um..." Twiddling her thumbs, Neo pulled in a deep breath. "I'm sorry it took so long."

Brushing her cheek with my thumb, I told her, "I'd wait for you forever."

Our lips were like magnets, drawn to one another. Our

centers too. But there was nothing slow and soft about our connection this time. She was ass up, clenching the sheets as she threw that ass back. Each medium paced stroke had her body smacking against mine as I reacquainted myself with her pussy. Between her whimpers, grunts, and moans... that shit was like a drug. A drug I wanted to consume every day for the rest of my life.

"This has been so much fun," Neo said, swirling her fingers around my chest.

After we made love, we went out on the town. I took her out for dinner, then we went to a popup museum that highlighted Black artists. We hadn't really talked about what this day was going to lead to, but I was grateful that she'd made her way back to me.

"I'm glad you enjoyed yourself. And I'm glad you came back to me."

"How have things been?"

"Good. Omar is gone to Atlanta, and he told her he'd be back when she had the baby, but I doubt it. We told Marz he's going to be a big brother, and he's happy about that. I've been looking into buildings for my training academy. I'm not rushing it, though, because I want it to be perfect."

"That's exciting. I've been looking at buildings and apartments too. I haven't seen anything yet that really caught my eye, so I'm being patient."

I made the mental note to get with Cooper about getting a commercial building for her. I didn't want her to stress over the financial process, and it was important to me that she be stable enough to never have to worry about anyone taking anything from her again. As much as I wanted to tell her she could stay with me, she'd shared with me that she rushed into moving in with Steven after he gave her the business.

"What are you looking for in buildings? And are you looking into particular areas?"

I listened intently as she ran down her list, locking in everything for future reference. Our conversation shifted. We continued to catch up, and she told me about her mom asking about our status earlier because of a cruise. I told her I didn't mind being her plus one. Aries and I took turns planning things for Marz for the summer anyway.

That caused me to ask her, "You plan on giving me more babies? I want like four."

"Four!" She shrieked before giggling and tossing her leg over me. "Baby, that's a lot."

"I know, but I want a big family since I was an only child."

"I feel you. I was the same way."

"Then what was your number?"

"Three."

"Aight, so how about you give me three, and with Marz, we will have four total."

"I think that sounds perfect."

After kissing her forehead, I asked, "How I'm supposed to love you?"

She looked up at me, and her smile made my heart skip a beat. "You mean like my love language?"

"Yeah, I guess, though I don't think anyone has just one way to feel loved."

"I can agree with that. I feel like saying I have just one boxes me in. I need different things at different times. Like... my parents were super generous because I was their only child, right? So from childhood, I'd say my love language is gifts. But as an adult, I started to feel loved more by men with quality time. Some days it's touch, and when I'm overwhelmed, it's service. Maybe I'm a greedy lover, but I want it all."

"That doesn't make you greedy. Even if you were, I have no problem keeping you satiated. I'm tryna feed your soul and make sure you never get up from my table because you feel empty. I want you to feast." Neo sat up and looked down at me. "What?"

"Who told you to say that?"

"Say what?"

"What you just said. Did my mom call you?"

Chuckling, I shook my head and lifted it slightly to give her a quick kiss. "No, baby. Why?"

"I was talking to my mom about you earlier, and she used me getting food poisoning as an analogy of why I shouldn't run away from you. She said I should let you be the chicken noodle soup for my soul and that I should feast. Then I asked for a God wink and your delivery arrived. Now, you're saying the exact same thing she said earlier."

"Well... maybe this conversation was His way of giving you exactly what you'd asked for."

"Maybe so."

She lowered herself to my lips, and we found ourselves connected at the center again. I could say we were making up for lost time, but that wasn't the case. I wanted this woman always in all ways—all day. Even if no time had passed, I'd still want to join her as one.

Three Weeks Later
Early April

When Aries asked me to hang out, I didn't know what to expect. Asia had never asked to spend time with me with Steven and China or alone. Looking back on that relationship, there were so many signs I missed. I could pinpoint the exact moment he started cheating on me, because it was also when China started to change.

At the beginning of our relationship, China and I were cool. She was sweet and respectful, and we had a great time together. After I moved in with Steven, she started acting more distant and closed off when she came around. I remember the day she got her report card, she just so happened to be at our house. Because she'd gotten a D in one of her classes, Steven took her phone.

He went through her text messages and saw that China had been talking big shit about the both of us with her mother. Asia had been planting seeds of discord between us, talking to China about me and my relationship with her father as if she was a grown woman. I appreciated the fact that Steven told her she had to respect me, regardless of what her mom said. After that, though, it was never the same.

Even though I tried to make a relationship with me and China work, I was paranoid and felt like she was never being sincere. All I could think about was how I was putting forth effort to bond with her and she was talking about me to her mother as soon as our time was over. I still tried to hang with her and make sure she felt comfortable around me, but I knew we'd probably never have the close bond I wished I'd have with my man's child.

Things were already different with Aries and Marz. Not just because Marz was younger but because Aries was putting forth the effort to get to know me. I kind of wanted to get inside her head about it, but I was also trying to trust that she had pure intentions. None of them deserved to deal with my paranoia and overthinking, so I was trusting my God wink and that I was truly safe with Merc.

We decided to go bowling, since that was something we could do that wouldn't require a lot of talking. After our second game, we started to loosen up more. I'd set the order of quesadillas I'd purchased us on the table as she said, "You're pretty cool. I see why Merc likes you."

"Thank you. You're pretty cool yourself. I'm glad bowling is something we both enjoy doing. Maybe we can make this a monthly thing until your belly gets too big for you to see over it."

Aries laughed as she nodded. "I'm down with that for sure. I'm a home body and don't go out too much, but I do love bowling and skating."

"Ooh, I love skating!"

"Yassss, we'll have to do that too then."

"For sure." I paused before asking, "What made you ask to do this?"

Her smile was warm as she chewed the piece of quesadilla that she'd just bitten. "I was waiting for you to ask me that." We shared a laugh. "I want to get to know the first woman Merc has had around our son. Based on how he feels about you, I think you'll be around for quite some time." That made my heart melt. "Also, I wanted to be able to tell you myself that there is absolutely nothing romantic between us. I know people can lie in your face about that kind of thing, but I don't want Merc's crazy ass. What we had is in the past, and we are not compatible at all. We're good friends and great parents to our son, but that's as far as it will ever go. You never have to worry about him cheating on you—with me or anyone else."

I didn't really know how much I needed this moment until she said those words. Standing, I walked over to her side of the table for a hug. This was the kind of thing I needed to feel safe with my man. I never wanted to have baby mama drama. A man with a child had an extra gift that came with him. One that I'd be able to provide with extra love. I wanted to be with a man whose baby mama understood and appreciated that, not felt threatened by it or want to push me away.

So far, things with Merc, Marz, and Aries were off to a really great start, and I was excited to see where they would go.

~

I WAS SO EMBARRASSED.

After we took Marz to Incredible Pizza, we chilled and

got ready to go out for karaoke with the crew. Merc was cross faded off weed and whiskey, and he'd decided to serenade me. The problem was, Merc was great at a lot of things, but singing wasn't one of them.

I couldn't stop laughing as he belted "Made for Me" by Muni Long at the top of his longs. I mean I was laughing so hard tears were in my eyes. Everyone around us laughed and recorded the scene, and I knew Innvy would send it to me before the night was over for me to cherish forever.

He took my hand into his and helped me to stand. We swayed with our arms wrapped around each other as he sang and I laughed. When the song was over, I think everyone was clapping so hard because he'd finally shut up. The microphone was quickly yanked from his hand, and that made me laugh harder.

"That was great, baby," I said as we sat back down.

"Aw yeah? You want an encore?"

"No!" I yelled a bit louder than I intended to, along with everyone else at our table. We all burst into a fit of laughter, and Merc did too after he flipped everyone off. This man was irreplaceable, and I was glad I decided not to let fear rule.

"Oh my God, baby." Neo's words were slurred.

"Shit," I moaned.

With her ankles by my shoulders, I was nestled deep in her pussy. Her walls gripped me tight. Each deep, shaky breath she took made my body shudder. Neo's lips and chin trembled as she unraveled underneath me. This time, I was unable to hold off, and I came right along with her.

Rolling off her, my chest heaved as I fought to catch my breath. If this was what I got after taking her on a date, I'd take her ass out every night. We'd gone to a cooking and wine pairing class that Antonne and Haley hosted and got a little wine tipsy. The moment we got to the house, she was all over me, and I had absolutely no complaints. Things between us had been perfect, and I knew they would only get better now that she was finally trusting me.

"You should move in," I blurted.

She didn't respond right away. A quiet snicker filled the air before she did. "Is that a post-sex declaration?"

"Yeah," I admitted with no hesitation, causing us both to laugh. "I did want you to move in, but I wasn't going to ask you to. I guess having such a good time with you this weekend made it difficult for me to hold it in. Plus, knowing you and Aries are building a bond and my little man is already crazy about you. He actually has a crush on you, and I'on wanna have to check him about that shit."

Neo laughed and straddled me. She put me back inside her pussy, causing me to moan and bite down on my bottom lip as I gripped her waist.

"Why weren't you going to ask me to move in?"

"Because I know you felt like you rushed moving in with Steven because of what he did for you. I didn't want you to question if moving in with me would lead to the same thing."

"Well, I..."

"I don't want you to answer," I interrupted her to say, pulling her down to my chest. "I want you to know that I want you here and that you can move in any time. It'll be your choice. Whenever you're comfortable, just come... and don't ever leave."

"Mm... I love the sound of that, baby." Her hand cupped my cheek, and she connected her lips with mine, moving against my still hard dick in the process. Pulling my hands behind my head, I relaxed and allowed her to take control, knowing I would enjoy every fucking second of it.

"I THINK I SHOULD MOVE OUT."

At the sound of Aries's statement, I lifted my head. I'd just finished helping Marz with his homework. Now, she was about to get him ready for dinner, which we'd eat together. We didn't always eat together, but since she'd cooked a large pot of spaghetti and fried fish, she invited me to join them. She'd tasked Marz with picking out what pajamas he wanted to put on, and I certainly wasn't expecting her to say that when we were alone.

"You want to move out?" I repeated. She nodded. "Okay, but why?"

"It's time, Merc. Your relationship with Neo is getting serious. Even though she and I are establishing a bond, I don't ever want her to feel like you do too much for me."

"Aries, Neo understands that the promise I made to you was established before she even came into the picture. She's not expecting me to stop taking care of you just because I'm with her."

"I know that, and I appreciate that, but still. Eventually, y'all are going to get married and have more babies and I... I don't want to be a burden, Merc."

"Aries..."

"I know you say I'm not, and I know we're a family, but be real. You can't take care of me forever."

"Yes, I can," I replied with a chuckle. "I'm not going to force you to take my money, but you don't have to move. I can see if you were living with me, but you're not."

Aries closed the space between us and took my hands into hers. "Tell me you don't take as great care of me as you do because you feel like you failed in our relationship." I couldn't respond right away. "Tell me you don't want me close because it allows you to still have the family dynamic you had growing up. Tell me that somewhere in that brain of yours, this isn't your way of having me as your wife so you can give our son the two-parent household you had and you believe he deserves, and I'll let you take care of me forever."

I couldn't say any of that because all of it was the truth. Because of the healthy upbringing I had with my parents, I wanted Marz to have the same. It broke my heart when Aries and I decided to break up, but I knew it was for the best. We were miserable, and I didn't want Marz to pick up on that. Having them right behind my home was perfect because it felt like we lived together but still had space. So while I had absolutely no romantic feelings for Aries, she was absolutely right. It meant more to me than anything to give my son the upbringing he deserved, even if I had to stay single to do it. Now, I'd fucked around and fallen in love with Neo, and I couldn't see my life without her.

"I can't tell you that, Aries," I admitted, causing her to smile and kiss my hands.

"I appreciate what you've done and will do for me and our son, but this is for the best, Merc. It won't be immediate, but it'll be by the end of the year. I know it would be silly of me to try and work now that I'm about to have another baby, but I do plan to put my tech background to use and find a work from home job. If it gets to be too much, I'll come back to the suite, but I need to do this, Merc, for all of us."

I knew there was no talking her out of this, so I nodded my agreement. "Aight, Aries. Let me at least pay your rent up for the first year so you can adjust comfortably."

"I can agree to that."

"I don't want y'all to go far."

"We won't. I won't be able to afford a house in your neighborhood, but I've been looking at apartments that are out this way, so he won't have to change schools."

"Or... you can let me buy you a house out this way, so you won't have to worry about rent or your mortgage. And this way, I won't have to worry about if you'll be able to take care of the kids." She didn't answer right away, and I appreciated that she was considering it. "You can pay the rest of your bills, and we can come up with a monthly amount that I'll give you for child support. But let me gift you with a home on behalf of my son and his baby brother or sister."

She released a shaky breath. "I'm too emotional for you to be saying things to make me cry."

As she caught her tears, I laughed and put some space between us. "Is that a yes?"

"Yes, it's a yes."

"Good. Thank you for letting me do this, and for doing what you think is best for me."

"Always."

"Okay, Mommy. I choose these ones!" Marz came bolting into the room with his favorite pair of Batman pajamas.

"I don't know why I even asked. I knew you were going to pick those," she said, scooping him up and placing kisses all over his face.

Even if Aries temporarily lost herself with Omar, I'd never deny that she was a great mom. I didn't mind going above and beyond for her because of how hard she went for our son.

One Month Later
Early May

I WAS an emotional wreck in the best way. When I told Merc about Heaven Can Wait, I wasn't expecting him to bring me here. But he had... and it was just as beautiful as it was on social media. Merc rented all four king suites. There were lounge areas in every room along with fireplaces. There was a home theater, jacuzzi, and infinity pool that overlooked the ocean. We even had a private beach. I was truly in awe of such a beautiful creation.

We'd just finished our catered breakfast which was phenomenal. Even though I was supposed to be getting dressed so we could start our day, all I could do was stare out into the beautiful view. At the feel of Merc's arms wrapping around me from behind, I melted against him.

"Is it as beautiful as you thought it would be?" he asked.

"Even more. And the fact that I get to share it with you

makes it all the more perfect. Thank you for bringing me here, baby."

"You're welcome. I figured a beautiful moment of telling you that I love you for the first time and asking you to commit to me deserved a beautiful scenery."

Turning in his arms, my mouth hung open until I smiled. With a giggle, I wrapped my arms around him.

"I love you too, and I would love to commit to you, Mercury."

"Good. Not that you had much of a choice." Between his teasing tone and playful smile, I couldn't help but laugh.

"You really brought me all the way across the world to tell me you love me and ask me to be your woman? I can't wait to see what you do when you ask a woman to be your wife."

Merc licked his lips before placing a kiss on mine. "Give me about six months to a year, and you'll find out."

Two Weeks Later

I DIDN'T WANT to get my hopes up, so I kept my excitement down. Merc was confident that I'd like the building Cooper recommended for my store. It had been torture not being open, but I was serious about taking my time and finding the right building. I wanted something that would not only be great for my inventory but for events as well.

"Aight, so this building is in a safer location than your last store..."

"Which means it's going to be more expensive," I interrupted him to say.

He chuckled and bobbed his head. "Yeah, but I think it's worth it."

"Mhm," I said, making him laugh again.

I'd planned to get a loan to help continue to build my credit. I was in the mid-700s which I was very proud of. When I did decide to move, my options would be limitless. Getting a loan would also allow me to keep the money I'd saved to put toward traveling and my move.

Still, I trusted Merc. I told him what I was looking for and what I wanted to spend comfortably, so I didn't think he'd have me getting excited about something I wouldn't be able to afford.

When we arrived in front of the building, I couldn't deny how impressed I was. It was a large red brick building. It was in Cordova. Some parts of Cordova were starting to go down, but not this area. It was still safe and filled with lots of stores and restaurants that could lead to traffic for my store.

We got out of his car and spoke to Cooper who congratulated me in advance because he was sure I'd like what I saw.

I did.

The building had three levels.

Merc suggested I used the second level for the store, the first level for events, and the third level as my apartment.

It was so perfect I wanted to cry.

"Baby, I love this, but there's no way I can afford it. I don't want to spend more than forty-five hundred a month."

"What if I told you that you only had to pay me with

your love." His arms wrapped around me, and he gave me a soft, tender kiss.

With a moan, I wrapped my arms around his neck. "Although I love the sound of that, I'm not sure that's how real estate works."

Merc gave me a sexy chuckle and licked his lips. "That's how it works when ya man buys you this building." A clipped whimper escaped me as my head shook. "And before you tell me no, the building will be in your name. It's all yours. Regardless of what happens between us, no one will ever be able to take your store away from you again."

Running my tongue over my teeth didn't stop my tears from falling.

"Neo," he said softly, and that only made me cry harder. "Baby." Merc chuckled as he picked me up and held me close. "Why you cryin'?"

"Why are you doing this for me?"

"Because I love you." He kissed my tears away. "You're my woman, soon my wife. That makes you my responsibility, and I'm going to always make sure you have everything you want and need."

Resting my forehead against his as I sniffled, I rubbed my hand down the back of his head.

"I can really have this?"

"You can really have this."

"Thank you, baby, it's perfect." Cupping his cheeks, I pecked his lips until he smiled. "You're perfect."

"No, I'm not, far from it, but I am perfect for you."

Our lips connected again, and I kissed him until my excitement and happiness surged and released as a laugh. Merc put me down, and I looked at each level all over again. Now that I knew it was mine, the space was brighter and filled with even more potential. Already, ideas were pouring over how I could utilize the event space. I didn't think Merc could do anything to top taking me to South Africa to ask me to be his, but gifting me this perfect building for my store came close. And the crazy thing was, I felt nothing that I did when Steven did the same thing.

This felt pure.

This felt right.

This felt like unconditional love.

Six Months Later
Thanksgiving

As I looked around the dining room, I was truly a proud and content man.

My family, Neo's family, and our friends were in attendance for Thanksgiving dinner. I loved that our parents got along so well.

A lot had changed, and a lot of things remained the same.

Aries had given birth to a beautiful baby girl who she named Ariel, and Marz was obsessed with his little sister. He was adjusting to being in first grade and was still locked in with Kiana.

They were cute.

Aries did move out, and the house was about a mile away. She'd allowed me to purchase it for her, and Marz loved it because it had a pool.

I'd found a building for my training academy and

planned to start accepting students at the start of the new year. Bully and Innvy were engaged and going strong. Her little round belly was cute. I thought it was dope that she and Neo were pregnant at the same time. Not only would our kids be able to grow up with Marz, but Bully, Asylum, and I would all have babies to raise together.

Neo had been staying in the apartment at the top of the building while she and her associate, Moriah, got the store together. When we found out she was pregnant with my little lady, she agreed to move in. Steven had reached out to her when word began to spread about her new store. He was shocked taking the first one didn't make her stay, and even more shocked when I had Toe pay him a visit. After that, Neo didn't have any more problems out of him. Apparently, he and his baby mama still hadn't officially gotten back together, but they were still living with each other. More power to them with that toxic, cliché ass shit.

Rey was still a heavy presence in Neo's life. She spent a day or two with him every week, playing the keyboard for him while he continued to teach her Chess. He'd joined us for dinner this evening, and I was grateful for that.

All in all, all was well in my life. The only thing that was going to make it better was Neo agreeing to be my wife. I planned to take her back to the cabin before Christmas to do that, and there was no doubt in my mind that she would say yes. As if she felt herself on my mind and in my heart, she made her way over to me with tired eyes and a wide smile. Though the women insisted she and Innvy didn't have to do anything, they along with Dauterive acted like they just couldn't sit still.

As she made herself comfortable on my lap, I wrapped my arms around her.

"You look happy," she noticed.

"I'm happier than I ever thought was possible, and you have a hell of a lot to do with that."

My hand went to her stomach. As if my little lady knew my touch, she instantly started to move.

"Look at her showing out for Daddy."

"You gon' show out for Daddy later too?"

As I placed kisses along her neck, she giggled. "You know I'm always down for that."

Neo lifted my face by my chin and covered my lips with hers. I moaned against them, willing my dick not to get hard, but that was always hard to do. I loved everything about this woman and was so attracted to her she could get me painfully hard with the slightest touch. And it wasn't just on some sexual shit. It was the fact that my body and my heart wanted to make sure I knew she was the only woman they wanted me to ever connect with.

Christmas Eve

"You know what would be crazy?" Neo said as I pulled into the driveway of the cabin. "If we got snowed in again."

"Yeah, that would be crazy as hell. I wouldn't mind it, but Marz would lose his shit if we weren't back by Christmas."

"Boy, please. Marz won't care about you not being there. He still gon' open his gifts."

I laughed because she was absolutely right. "I know. That's why he can't do it without me. I let him believe in Santa, but I still like to see him open his things, even though he immediately forgets about me to go play for the rest of the day."

She laughed as I got out and grabbed our bags then opened the door for her. Her stomach had gotten even bigger over the last month. It was crazy that she'd gotten pregnant while on birth control. I had no complaints about it. Our little lady was made in love, and I was going to be just as present with her as I was with Marz. Neo and Aries were sure I'd spoil my little lady more, and I wouldn't deny that. She was going to soften me and Marz and be spoiled by us just like Ariel was.

As soon as we walked into the cabin, Neo gasped and whimpered. I'd had an event planner to come and set everything up on my behalf. I could have waited until we got here and did it myself, but I would have been too anxious. As far as I was concerned, I'd waited long enough to make Neo my fiancée.

I wanted to take her to another country to propose, but since she was so far along in her pregnancy, I decided to bring her back to the place where things changed for us.

Neo looked back at me, twisting her mouth to the side as her eyes watered. I took her hand and led her down the aisle of white rose petals. Instead of red, I requested white —white roses, white balloons and candles, white garland and banner—white everything.

"Baby," she whispered, gripping my hand.

Kneeling, I turned her slightly so that she was facing me. For a moment, I got lost in her beauty. She'd been wearing a lot of dresses because they were most comfortable against her belly. The white sweater dress she had on with white heels and gold accessories made her look ethereal. Her locs were pulled into a petal crown. Golden makeup accented her natural beauty.

Damn.

I was a lucky... blessed... man.

Pulling the ring I'd gotten from her father out of my pocket, I told her, "Your mother and father gave me this with their approval. I had it upgraded and resized to fit you." Pausing, I pulled in a deep breath. All my confidence flew out the window momentarily. For a split second, I got nervous as hell. Chuckling, I shook away my nerves. "I love you, Neo. You're not just a great addition to my life and family; you're the crown. On top of your presence, you're gifting me with a precious princess that I can't wait to welcome into this world and fill with so much love.

"But I dare not do that before making her mother my wife. So will you do me the greatest honor of marrying me? Will you be my wife?"

Tears streamed down her cheeks as she nodded. Giggling, she wiped her face with her free hand.

"Yes, Mercury! Of course!"

My grin spread as I slid the ring on her finger. With a moan, I felt weightless as I stood. Taking her into my arms, I kissed her deeply. I didn't think it would ever happen... but Neo tamed the gangsta and made me her forever gentleman.

Neo

The Weekend After Christmas

I was so uncomfortable in my own body. I couldn't wait to have my baby. The fact that I was even pregnant right now was crazy to me. We certainly weren't trying, so I knew my baby was a gift from God. At thirty-two weeks pregnant, I felt I was slightly prepared. Dauterive had her baby two months ago, and Aries had hers four months ago. Innvy and I were pregnant at the same time, and I think that was what made this most special.

Neither Merc nor I wanted to fly for the babymoon, so he asked me where I wanted to go that was within driving distance. After I had the baby, he told me he would take me anywhere in the world. I'd finally decided where I wanted to go, and when I went to find him and tell him, I got the shock of my life.

It wasn't just the fact that he was sitting behind his piano playing, praying, and worshipping God. It was the fact that he was praying over our baby's sonogram. And his voice was so beautiful. I thought he couldn't sing because of how horrible he sounded that night for drunk karaoke, but Merc had a beautiful voice.

Tears immediately filled my eyes as he ran his fingers over the sonogram and thanked God for our baby girl. I didn't think there was a side to this man that could surprise me at this point, but I was happy and honored to be wrong. I was truly the luckiest woman alive to be with Mercury. He was the perfect mix of nasty and sweet, kind and rough, gangster yet gentle... and spiritual yet savage as fuck.

Wiping my tears, I walked into our music room with a smile on my face that nothing would be able to wipe off. I wrapped my arms around his neck and placed a kiss on his cheek near the corner of his mouth. With a smile of his own, Merc placed me on his lap and continued to play and sing. He led my hands to the piano, and I continued his melody as he rubbed my belly and hummed against my neck. Hums turned into kisses that made me squirm and giggle as I thanked God for this amazing change in my life.

The End

Up next:
Beethoven
To preorder: Click here.

These characters have their own books. To read, click below.
Asylum and Dauterive
The Mister Series:
Kahlil and Honey

Elite (Supreme and Nicole) and Denali
Hosea and Cartier
Saint and Harmony
Tyreek and Janae
Antonne and Haley

LET'S CONNECT!

Mailing list - https://bit.ly/MLBLove22
On all social media - @authorblove
If you rave about this book on TikTok, tag me, and let's make a duet!
For exclusive eBooks, paperbacks, and audiobooks – www.prolificpenpusher.net

As always, if you enjoyed this book, please leave a review on Amazon/Goodreads, recommend it on social media and/or to a friend, and mark it as READ on your Goodreads profile.

Follow B. on Amazon for updates on her releases by clicking here.

By the Book with B. Podcast – bit.ly/bythebookwithb

TRADITIONALLY PUBLISHED BLP AUTHORS

An emotionally charged psychological thriller that will leave fans breathless as they bear witness to the lengths a wife will go to honor her vows. An addictive page turner for fans of twisty plots in the same vein of Colleen Hoover's *Verity*.

Perfect wife... Perfect life... until you can't remember either.

The moment Dante Williams wakes up on the side of

the road, unsure of where he is or who he is, his life changes for the worse. After a brief stay in the hospital, Dante is released to the care of his loving wife, Sade. Sade is beautiful, successful, and loyal. So loyal, she devotes herself to Dante indefinitely, hoping this will help him appreciate what he has—his life and his wife.

While seemingly having it all, their perfect marriage isn't enough to keep Dante from digging up the past in hopes of recovering his memory. It isn't long before he begins questioning Sade's behavior and intentions. Once secrets start to unravel, Dante is left more confused than the day following the accident.

When Dante discovers evidence of something more sinister at play, he prepares to end his marriage but learns quickly that Sade meant every word in her vows and plans to honor them, until *death*.

Available as an eBook, audiobook, and paperback. To purchase at any major retailer: https://www.authorblove.net/the-loyal-wife

Two decades ago, two strangers make a connection that bonds them for life. Perfect for fans of second chance romance, This Time Around is the love reunion hopeless romantics have been waiting for.

Dr. Tessa Howard is sick and tired of everything—her job, her nagging mother, and her boyfriend who wouldn't know commitment if it hit him in the face. The only thing that didn't work her last nerve was her soon-to-be twenty-year-old daughter, Cyrah. Watching her one and only child, her greatest accomplishment, live life out loud was her greatest joy. Tessa didn't know what she'd do if she didn't have Cyrah, whom she admittedly lived vicariously through. After an epiphany in the middle of the night, Tessa finds herself single and unemployed. With no job, no man, and no prospects for either, Tessa finally decides to let loose and learns that history does, in fact, repeats itself.

Dr. Cypress Boone recently ended a relationship after a two-year engagement. He'd given his all to Emery, but she played him for a fool. Although disappointed, he hasn't given up on love and is ready for a fresh start. Emery, however, isn't ready to let go and refuses to accept that they are over. In an effort to make a clean break, he accepts a job at the prestigious Black Elm University, over two thousand miles away from his current residence. With a new job in a new city, Cypress has high hopes that a new woman will soon be added to the equation. However, maybe this time around, someone new isn't what he needs.

To purchase at any major retailer: https://linktr.ee/kayshanee

To purchase at any major retailer: https://mailchi.mp/a0a334b6e4ce/courage-to-love-again-paperback-preorders

Pascha St. Claire has nothing to live for.

After five years, her once-loving husband, Raymond, decides to end their marriage. He's unable to deal with her mental health, significant weight gain, or the idea that she cannot seem to birth him a child. She returns home one night to find her belongings on the curb and the locks to her home changed. Her pleading falls on deaf ears as Raymond has made the decision to end their marriage. With no other option, Pascha is forced to leave and never look back.

When Callum Ellis accepted the reservation for his car service, the last thing he expected was to pick up a beautiful, weeping stranger. His heart goes out to her as he drops her off at a hotel. After discovering her credit cards have been canceled, Callum swoops in to pay for her stay. Though she wants to protest, Pascha realizes she is in no position to decline the stranger's generous offer.

Months roll by and Callum is still unable to get Pascha out of his head. A chance encounter finally lands him in her presence, and Callum is determined to make the most of it. Though she initially declines his interest, Pascha soon finds herself intrigued by the once-kind stranger. Fear has her recoiling at his advances, but men like Callum come to restore. Will Pascha continue to avoid the inevitable, or does she find the courage to love again?

Coming 2025!

"If loving you is wrong, I don't want to be right."

Talia Tate has been given the case of a lifetime. With the entire world tuned in to find out if the novice lawyer for Tate & Associates could get a not guilty verdict in the State V. Duncan trial, Talia is stressed and determined to prove to the world, her bosses, and herself that she is a brilliant lawyer worthy of respect. However, there is one person standing in her way of success.

Detective Maddox Reed doesn't mind cutting corners when it comes to closing a case. Since his days in patrol, the locals knew to steer clear of "Speedy Reed-y." When Donovan Duncan was brought into his squad room, he was ready to send him to prison without an interrogation. He thought the case was cut and dry... Until Talia comes to his office with fingers pointed ready to get Donovan the justice he deserved.

To be on opposite sides of the law, Talia and Maddox find themselves fighting two battles: justice and lust. How could they fall in love under circumstances so polarizing the whole world can feel the tension? While both of them are in a race to come out on top, surprising feelings make it difficult to separate business from pleasure. Will these two souls find solace with one another? Or will the burden of love be too hard to bear?

ALSO BY B. LOVE

Standalone Romance

Love Me Until I Love Myself (Christian Romance)

Give Me Something I Can Feel

Saving All My Love for You

To Take: A Novella

In Haven

Weak: An Irresistible Love

The Ashes: The Medina Sisters' Story

Just Say You Love Me

If You Ever Change Your Mind #1

Coffee with a Side of You #1

If He Loves Me #1

In Due Time #1

Will You Still Want Me? #1

If You'll Let Me

Til Morning #1

I'll Be Bad For You #1

Just Love Me (Shenaé Hailey)

Due for Love (Shenaé Hailey)

Til I Overflow

Flesh, Flaws, and All (Christian romance)

Make it Last

Straddling His Soul #1

Fingers on his Soul

My Love Wasn't Meant for You

The Preying Pastor

Everything I Desire

Someone She Loved #1

Give Me Love

Love Me for Christmas

Trapped Wishes #1

Yours to Have #1

Unequivocally, Blindly, Yours

Brief Intermission

But Without Haste #1

Last Chance to Love #1

Strumming My Pain #1

With His Song #1

Held Captive by a Criminals Heart #1

Fans Only

To Protect & Swerve

Now Playing: Reel Love

Faded Love

Just Like I Want You

Lie in It

April's Showers

The Mourning Doves

Finding a Wife for My Husband

In The Lonely Hour

Ours for Hours

Loving the Lonely

A Valentine for Christmas

The Love Dealer

The Love List

Santa's Cummin' to Town #1

Holly's Jolly Christmas

Bloody Fairy

Who Do You Love? - website exclusive.

His Sleeping Beauty #1

Asylum #1

Merc

The Boss Babe Series

Tampering with Temptation

Hungry for Her

Seducing a Savage

The Office Series

Her Exception 1: An Enemies to Lovers Romance

Her Exception 2: A Friends to Lovers Romance

Her Exception 3: A Fake Relationship Romance

The Hibiscus Hills Standalone Series

A Picture Perfect Love

The Mister Series

Mister Librarian #1

Mister: The Mister Series Prelude

Mister Jeweler #1

Mister Concierge #1

Mister Musician #1

Mister Teacher #1

Mister Sommelier

Banking on Love Series

60 Days to Love

The Business of Lust

Majority Rules #1

Romance Series

Love Me Right Now (1-2) #1

To Take: Crimson Trails series (1-5)

Send me (part 1) I'll go (part 2) #1

*The Love Series – The Love We Seek, The Love We Find, The Love We Share

Harts Fall Series – With All My Heart, With All My Trust, With All My Love (Shenaé Hailey)

Her Unfaithful Husband, His Loyal Wife, Their Impenetrable Bond (Shenaé Hailey)

Love is the Byline

Love's battleground

Love's garden #1

Ode to Memphis

Love Letters from Memphis

The Streets Will Never Love Me Like You Do

A Memphis Gangsta's Pain

In the Heart of Memphis

Rose Valley Hills (Standalones)

Sweet

Chapel

Steeped in his Love

Standalone Urban

To Be Loved by You

His Piece of Peace #1

Her Piece of Peace

Her piece of peace: The Wedding

Hunter and Onyx: An Unconventional Love Story - website exclusive.

Thief #1

A Hustler's Heaven in Hiding

His thug love got me weak

If I Was Ya Man

A Gangsta's Paradise #1

LoveShed

Kisses for my Side Mistress

Set Up for Love

Promise to Keep it Trill

Her Heart, His Hood Armor

Her Gangster, The Gentleman

Her Only Choyce

Let it H*E (Constance)

Yours to Keep

A Thug in Need of Love

Black Mayhem Mafia Family Saga

In His Possession

Her Deep Reverence

A Heart's Rejection

Under His Protection #1

A Father's Objection

In His Possession 2

A Heart's Connection

Indiscretion #1

Succession #1

Resurrection #1

Interception - website exclusive.

Gucci Gang Saga

I Need A Gangsta

One Love

Urban Series

She Makes the Dopeboys go Crazy (1-2) - website exclusive.

Caged Love: A Story of Love and Loyalty (1-5)

If You Give Me Yours (part 1) I'll Give You Mine (part 2) #1

Loved by a Memphis Hoodlum 3

It Was Always You 2

The Bad Boy I Love 2

No Love in His Heart 3

My Savage and His Side Chick 2

So Deep In Love

Faded Mirrors

Behind Every Great Gangsta - website exclusive.

Beginning Career Titles

(Series are separated. Characters are overlapped. These titles do not have to be read together, but if you'd prefer to know what stories everyone is from, you can read them in this order. ***Power and Elle and Rule and Camryn can be read alone without reading anything else.****)*

Kailani and Bishop: A Case of the Exes 1-3

Alayziah: When Loving him is Complicated 1-2

Teach Me how to Love Again 1-2

—

Power and Elle: A Memphis Love Story

Rule and Camryn 1-4: A Memphis Love Story

Femi (Spinoff for Rule and Camryn)

—

Young Love in Memphis 1-3

But You Deserve Better

Made in the USA
Columbia, SC
02 July 2024